MW00949369

Printed in the United States of America

Burton Crown, 2016

ISBN-13:978-1530061839

ISBN-10:1530061830

www.hannahschrock.com

Book One: Amish Doubt

And Jesus answered them, "Truly, I say to you, if you have faith and do not doubt, you will not only do what has been done to the fig tree, but even if you say to this mountain, 'Be taken up and thrown into the sea,' it will happen. - Matthew 21:21

Bopplis. Emma Bontrager almost slipped on the ice hidden beneath the fresh, afternoon snow as she walked down the road to Emile Smith's retired *Englisch* farm. She knew she should focus on conquering the treacherous slope with her basket full of goodies, but *bopplis, bopplis, bopplis* pervaded her thoughts.

"Sarah is so round!" Martha exclaimed from up ahead, "Round like a pumpkin! Isn't that right, Emma?"

Emma stopped for a moment, readjusting her woolen coat over her dress and stockings. Martha turned back to look at her, waiting for a reaction, her bright blue eyes blinking the falling snowflakes off of her thick lashes.

At fifteen, Martha would soon approach her *rumspringa* years, the time at which Amish teenagers explored and experienced the world before pledging themselves to the Church. Her question about the physical aspects of their elder sister's third trimester pregnancy made perfect sense with her growing fascination with physical looks, despite the fact that their family did not allow any mirrors or photographs in order to promote humility.

"*Ach*, what should it matter what she will look like?" Emma asked her sister. "A baby is a gift from *Gott*, Martha, we should be excited for what this means for Sarah and Jeremiah."

"*Ja*," Eli offered, throwing the snowball he had been forming in his gloved hands for the past five minutes. It hit Martha in the stomach, scattering the snow across her dark coat and skirts and making her giggle. "It isn't good to think of *Gott's* gifts in such a manner, little one."

Martha brushed at the snow clinging to her clothes, sticking out her tongue at Eli affectionately. He made to chase her, making her squeal as she bounded a few steps down the hill, her own basket swinging in one hand.

Emma suddenly felt glad that Eli had come along. He looked over at her, as if reading her thoughts, giving her a familiar crooked smile. A cap sat atop his sandy blonde hair, and snowflakes had settled on the strands. He had gotten the day off from his job at the *Englisch* farm near town, and had eagerly agreed to help Emma and Martha bring their goods to Mr. Smith. Emma knew how her sister looked up to Eli; she hoped his good influence would rub off on Martha, who was clearly experiencing her first thoughts of vanity.

"Soon you'll join the Church and you and Eli will have lots of babies, too!" Martha said, after a few seconds of silence.

"Hush, Martha, there will be no talk of such things," Emma said, turning red at the mention of Eli in that way.

Eli laughed at the comment, threatening to throw another snowball at Martha, who grinned. Emma could never understand how certain things didn't upset him as they did her, especially when it came to their relatively new courtship. They had grown up together, attending church and community functions together from a young age, but this new side of their relationship confused and excited her. In addition to his fair features, Eli had generous heart and social nature in contrast to Emma's dark features and shy demeanor. He was her first beau, perhaps even her first love, though she wasn't sure yet.

Even if she did enjoy Eli's company, having shared his buggy on many occasions as they sipped hot chocolate and talked the night away, she wasn't ready to think about babies, more or less joining the Church. Although she was sure she wanted to remain Amish, and although she had almost reached the age of twenty-two, something always held her back from agreeing to baptism. Eli had already joined, and although she could tell he didn't want to pressure her, the look in his eyes when she mentioned it told her exactly what he wanted her to do.

For the Lord GOD will help me; therefore shall I not be confounded: therefore have I set my face like a flint, and I know that I shall not be ashamed. - Isaiah 50:7

Barking greeted them as they neared the edge of Mr. Smith's long driveway, which had been plowed even though he could not drive himself. Martha giggled as the man's dog, Snip, ran up to her, licking her gloved hands and stuffing his nose into the basket.

"Not for you, silly boy!" Martha said, laughing still as she raised her basket, scratching one of Snip's ears and making his tail wag so hard that even Emma had to smile.

"Bring *der hund* and let's go," Emma said, "My nose is about to fall off from the cold."

Martha obeyed, calling Snip along as they climbed the driveway, trudging through the freshly plowed snow. To either side of the drive, old tractors and equipment laid scattered about, rusting in the damp cold. Emma always felt a chill run down her spine as she approached the old farm. Although the place had clearly once been a thriving dairy establishment, Emile's children had all moved and his wife of fifty years had passed away, leaving him, an old man, living alone. When they had ran into Emile at the supermarket a little over two years ago, *Daed* and *Mamm* had instantly taken a liking to him, and had been sending him meals every Saturday ever since, despite the mile distance between their houses.

Today, a big red pickup sat in the driveway. Emma paused for a moment, exchanging a glance with Martha, since the vehicle could not have been Mr. Smith's and did not belong to his *Englisch* neighbor, who usually plowed his driveway for him, either.

Eli, who had never met Mr. Smith, peered at the truck. Working at a modern farm had given him more knowledge about automobiles and equipment than most Amish people, but Emma soon found that he wasn't looking at the truck to see what kind it was.

"I know who owns that truck," he said, surprising her.

In that moment, the door to the old farmhouse swung open and the sound of men's laughter filled the air. Emma again exchanged a glance with Martha. Neither of them had ever heard Mr. Smith laugh. At first, Emma had hated bringing food to the gruff old man, but *Mamm* had explained that Emile had been hardened by years of hardship and age. It was *Gott's* plan, she said, to put the man in their lives.

Mr. Smith leaned heavily on his cane as he walked out, his laughter dying when he saw them. Deep wrinkles surrounded his eyes, carved down into his neck and hunched shoulders. A single suspender held up his pants over a dirty white t-shirt.

"What are you doing here?" he asked, rather loudly, since he was hard of hearing.

Emma felt her face grow red in shame, but Martha answered, speaking loudly enough for the half-deaf man to hear her. "We're here to bring you..." her voice wavered, stopping completely.

A young *Englischer*, dressed in a red plaid shirt and blue jeans, had followed out after Mr. Smith. He had tousled auburn hair, with soft freckles that shrunk and grew with his smile. His smile, though, his smile made Emma blush even more.

"Better be nice to them, Emile, looks like they've brought you some good stuff." The man's voice, in contrast to the old man's gravelly undertone, seemed to soothe the situation. His eyes were fixed on Emma; she could feel him watching her even though she trained her eyes on the ground.

"*Ja*, see? I knew it!" Eli said to Emma, excited. "Hello, Jarron."

The stranger, Jarron, moved his gaze to Eli. His face lit up with a smile. "Eli Yoder, how are you?"

"Wonderful-good," Eli said, and in a few strides he had reached Jarron. The two men shook hands. "Jarron's *Daed* owns the farm where I work, and Jarron owns the red truck," Eli explained to the girls.

Jarron stood almost a head taller than Eli. Emma couldn't imagine the two working side-by-side. She realized he walked toward her now, holding out a big hand.

"Jarron Williams," he said. She glanced at his hand, then at his face, feeling her own hands grow sweaty.

Her tongue felt like lead in her mouth, but whether that was because of Mr. Smith, who was watching them all, or because of this stranger, Jarron, she didn't know.

"Martha," Martha said, nudging Emma's leg with her boot, taking the offered hand with courage and her best smile. "Martha Bontrager, and this is my sister..."

"Emma," Emma managed, as Jarron shook her sister's hand. For some reason she felt a spark of anger at Martha for answering for her, the older sister.

Jarron laughed, finally pulling his hand away from Martha's, though she looked like she didn't want to let it go.

"*Leuk je te ontmoeten*," he said, and Martha giggled at his pronunciation. "Did I say that wrong?"

"You said it just fine," Martha said, laughing. "For an *Englischer*, that is."

He smiled again. "Well, I try. Eli's taught me a little bit of Pennsylvania Dutch — right, Eli?"

Emma wanted to sink into the floor, embarrassed at her sister's boldness. Jarron seemed to sense her discomfort, turning back to talk with Eli and Mr. Smith, who was beginning to speak to Eli with interest.

The girls made their way into the house, greeted with its familiar scents. Emma set her basket on the table, fingers fumbling as she laid out a homemade apple pie and some store-bought peanuts, Mr. Smith's favorite. Martha unloaded her own basket, speaking under her breath.

"Jarron is so tall! And handsome!" she said.

"He's *Englisch*," Emma replied, uncomfortable with the conversation.

As they walked outside, carrying their empty baskets, Jarron held the door open for them. Emma tried to smile at him, but the curious way in which he looked at her made her nervous.

"I think Emile likes Eli," he said, winking at Emma. "It might take a while to pull him away."

Indeed, the men seemed to have taken an interest in each other. Eli spoke animatedly, using his hands to speak as he always did.

"Is that your red truck?" Martha blurted, earning a disapproving glance from Emma. Jarron drew his attention away from Emma. "It's so shiny!"

"It's my baby," he said, with pride. "A lot of time and effort and a little money goes a long way. I've had her for four years now."

He paused, looking like he had fallen into some sort of memory. Suddenly, he shook his head.

"Well, I suppose you don't really care about that, being Amish and all ... Meaning no offense," he said, smiling slightly.

Martha shrugged. "I'm almost sixteen," she said, clearly proud of her own statement. "I haven't been baptized yet. Neither has she," she said, pointing to Emma, as if accusing her of some grave sin. "She's getting old, though."

"Martha..." Emma gasped, feeling as if she was going to burst through her clothes with embarrassment. Martha didn't pay attention. Her eyes were on Jarron.

Jarron Williams, on the other hand, looked amused. "She doesn't look that old to me."

"She is," Martha affirmed, and Emma could feel tears of hurt sting her eyes. She didn't know why her sister would speak so negatively of her in front of this *Englischer*.

"You're not a day over eighteen, are you?" he asked Emma directly.

"She's almost twenty-two!" Martha interjected.

"Why, that's not old at all!" Jarron retorted, giving Martha a frown, "If she's old, I must be ancient! I'm twenty-four!"

The statement silenced Martha, who looked at him in awe. It was true that Jarron had a boyish look to him, but no doubt Martha felt exhilarated by the fact that Jarron seemed genuinely interested in what she, a fifteen-year-old, had to say.

Emma blinked the tears away from her eyes, trying to give him a grateful look. His eyes were still fixed on Martha, though.

"Well, we'd best be getting back home," Eli said, politely, giving Emma a glance.

"Oh, bah! Leave an old man to his misery!" Mr. Smith said, waving them away.

"Don't worry Emile, I'll be back," Jarron said, walking over to shake the old man's hand and pat him on the back, "Thanks for the conversation. I'll bring a beer next time."

Mr. Smith laughed. "You're a good man, Jarron. A good man!"

"We'll be off too, Mr. Smith," Emma said, finally able to find her tongue now that the strange young man's gaze had stopped watching her. "*Goede dag*, good day, sir."

That day, as the Bontragers and Eli marched home, with Martha raving about Jarron's physical appearance and Emma still slightly cross with her sister for her negative comments, Jarron Williams drove to town, wondering which of the seven Amish houses on the route belonged to them.

No temptation has seized you except what is common to man. And God is faithful; he will not let you be tempted beyond what you can bear. But when you are tempted, he will also provide a way out so that you can stand up under it. - Corinthians 10:13

Sarah's screams filled her house, piercing through the hot air and landing uncomfortably on everyone's eardrums.

Emma could hear Mam and Katie Yoder, who was helping with the birth, speak to each other over Sarah's sobbing. She couldn't tell if their voices sounded concerned, or if they were simply trying to keep quiet.

Sarah's husband, Jeremiah, stood in the corner of the outer room, shifting his weight from side to side, stroking his beard nervously at every sound. Martha sat in the opposite corner, uncharacteristically silent, tears in her eyes as she tried to continue knitting her stocking, a project she'd been working on for nearly a day since they'd heard that Sarah had entered labor. *Daed* sat next to Martha in a wooden chair, completely motionless, only moving once in a while to readjust his position. Emma took comfort from her father; he knew how to trust the Lord, how to keep calm in the midst of crisis.

She, too, sat still, but her thoughts felt guilty as she reflected, not for the first time, on the incident at Emile Smith's farm a couple weeks ago. On many levels, Martha's words to the *Englischer*, Jarron, had hurt and angered her. Why *hadn't* she joined the Church yet? The more she thought about it, the less she understood about her decision. Perhaps her heart didn't feel ready enough, perhaps she wasn't strong enough for the commitment her baptism would entail. She had tried to ask *Gott*, but he had been characteristically silent, offering no solution to the dilemma.

All she knew, all she could be sure about, was that she wasn't, she couldn't possibly be, ready yet. The thought frightened her — what if she would never be ready? Eli had taken to saying that she was a wonderful-good woman, someone with a beautiful heart. He had pressed her lips up against her forehead last they had met, sealing the statement with a kiss. She might have loved him. But how could someone with a beautiful heart and in love continue to think such thoughts? Why could she not accept her place among the Amish forever, if not for herself, for him?

And then there was Jarron, the strange *Englischer* who had known Eli. Had she imagined his interest in her? She had gone over the scenario thousands of times, thinking that he surely had an *Englisch* girl who worked at a coffee shop, someone who he loved, or that perhaps she had had something on her face that he kept looking at that day. Nothing made sense.

As she stood, everyone looked at her.

"I need to go for a walk," she announced, looking at *Daed*, who simply nodded. She had spoken with him about her hesitation to join the Church, but even he could not relieve her anxiety in that matter.

Donning her winter gear, she ventured out into the cold air, leaving the scents and sounds of a live birth behind. The snow had stopped falling, and the horses over the pasture stared at her. She nodded to them cordially and headed toward the country road, treading carefully through the snow-strewn yard.

At the road, unprotected by the trees, the wind whipped at her clothes and face, tugging at her cap. She turned her back against it, walking forward, savoring the rich, clean scent of winter.

A horn honked. She turned around, startled out of her reprieve. A big, red truck grumbled along behind her, eventually coming to a stop beside her.

She found herself looking straight into Jarron Williams' eyes.

"Hi, Emma," he said, drawing out his words. His smile looked warm and gentle, sweet in the dim glow of the winter sun. "Fancy seeing you here."

"*Hallo* Mr... Jarron," she corrected herself, averting her eyes to look at the ground.

"A bit cold to be walking, don't you think?" he asked.

"*Ja*, but my sister is having a baby. It's been a long process," she admitted, blushing a little at the topic. "What are you doing out this way?

"Wow, that's exciting," he said, smiling. She could tell he was trying to meet her glance, but she didn't look up. "Another trip into town for me. Emile needed some dog food for ol' Snip."

She made herself look into his eyes, for a second. His smile brightened. "That's very kind of you," she said.

He shrugged. "My family's known him for a long time."

She smiled, a little. "*Gott* works through us all."

Jarron's face grew serious. He nodded.

"Want to hop in? I've got heat," he said suddenly. "Honestly, I don't know how you Amish women walk around in dresses all the time. Don't you ever get cold?"

She studied his face, but she could find only amusement and curiosity. She looked back at her sister's house, then back at him.

"I suppose a few minutes wouldn't hurt," she said.

He reached over and popped up the lock of the door, opening it. His truck smelled like its cracked leather seats mixed with another, not unpleasant, musk. Soft music played from the radio, almost indistinguishable.

"Stockings," she said, looking at him shyly. "That's how we keep warm."

He grinned, nodding. "Makes sense."

This is how it might have been, she thought, to have been born into the *Englisch* world. While she and Eli rode in his little carriage together with blankets, *Englischers* like Jarron rode around in big trucks with heat and music to keep them company.

She looked at Jarron, at his calloused hand poised over the gear shift, at his arm, dressed in an *Englisch* shirt with a collar. A few wisps of auburn hair had crept their way over the collar, curling against the fabric.

"Emma," Jarron said, not looking at her. "I was wondering, do you want to go for a ride?"

Somehow, Emma had leaned closer. She could smell the slight hint of mint on his breath. The truck rumbled beneath them, motor revving slightly. The leather felt strange and foreign against her hand as she flattened her fingers against it.

Suddenly she felt like the *Englisch* girl who worked at the coffee shop, a girl that Jarron would love. She had her hair cut, curled, and styled like the models in the magazines she saw at the supermarket, not parted down the center and tucked beneath her *kapp*. She wore jeans and lipstick and stayed out late with her friends and Jarron. She could imagine what his kisses and embraces felt like.

A fantasy, like the ones she used to have during the early years of her *rumspringa*. Only this time, she could enter this foreign world in a way that she had never done before.

Yet, as sweet as it all was, everything seemed unfamiliar. The *Englisch* world was staring her straight in the face, literally, and she didn't know if she had the courage to commit to it. Or, the courage not to commit to it. She thought of Eli, of his crooked smile, his warm hand on hers. He did not feel foreign, or strange. He loved her, and she felt that she could grow to love him.

In the distance, she could hear a shrill voice. Emma and Jarron both turned to find Martha running toward them, waving.

"It's a boy!" she cried, the tears that were in her eyes now streaming down her face, "A boy!"

Jarron offered his congratulations, and Emma reached over, grabbing his hand and giving it a squeeze. His face turned back toward hers, puzzled.

"*Denke*," she said, "Thank you, Jarron."

She got out of the truck, tucking Martha beneath her arm and guiding her back to the house, excited to see the new life Sarah had just brought into the world. They neared the house, listening to the exclamations of joy and praise coming from within.

She looked back, searching for the red truck, but it had driven away. She followed Martha into the house, and, for the first time, she felt like she was where she belonged.

For I know the plans I have for you, declares the Lord, plans for welfare and not for evil, to give you a future and a hope. Then you will call upon me and come and pray to me, and I will hear you. You will seek me and find me, when you seek me with all your heart. - Jeremiah 29:11-13

It was strange how those few moments in Jarron's truck helped clear Emma's mind of doubt. *Gott's* plan was shown to her and she felt joy like never before.

The Bontrager's held a celebration meal that evening, accompanied by the wonderful sound of a newly born *boppli's* cries. Martha was a bundle of uncontrollable excitement, she didn't know if she should eat or just go and stare at the *boppli.* When the desert was served, Shoofly Pie, their *mamm's* speciality Emma made her announcement. She told her *familye* that she was going to be baptized. Her mamm cried with joy and Martha ran around like a fool, leaping up the stairs and waking Sarah to tell her the *gut* news.

The following wedding season Emma and Eli were married. Emma hoped that before long she would be having a little *boppli* of her own.

Book Two: Amish Secret

Behold! I tell you a mystery. We shall not all sleep, but we shall all be changed, - 1 Corinthians 15:51

The old barn cat batted his black paws at Emma's skirt, trying to catch the fabric between his claws. Isaac laughed from her lap, tittering and cooing at the animal, trying to touch it with his sweaty, chubby fingers.

Emma Bontrager shooed the cat away, shifting Isaac from one leg to the other, attempting to find a comfortable position in the stifling heat. Around her, the church members milled about Bishop Amos Leander's *hauss*; women talked quietly with each other while trying to hold their children still, as men shook hands and spoke about the latest harvest of the summer. Almost every one of them fanned themselves with a hand or hat to ward against the summer heat.

The smell of freshly-baked bread, roasted pork, and apple pies had filled the stagnant air. Emma could spot some store-bought ice cream on the picnic table near where her Mamm sat, talking with Lizzie Graber, Emma's aunt.

"*Ach,* what I might give the good Lord for some wind," said Emma's older sister Sarah, as she approached. She held out her arms for Isaac, relieving Emma from his persistent wiggling. "Cheer up," she said to Emma, sitting down beside her, holding her son close. Both mother and child had dark features that were always accented in the summer sun, like Emma's own. "You don't look like a woman just married, sister. Are you feeling ill?"

"I am hardly a woman just married," Emma said, giving her sister a half-smile. "It's just the heat, it makes me cross."

"*Jah*," Sarah said, understanding, "This summer has been absolutely boiling. It makes Isaac cranky, too," she said, fondly, watching as Isaac took one of her fingers in his small grasp.

In the distance, she could see Daed talking with Bishop Amos, engaged in what looked to be an intense conversation. Daed, with his tall, stocky figure hovered over the smaller man, whose brow was furrowed slightly as he spoke. Her own husband, Eli Yoder, stood near the two men, listening with his arms crossed.

His beard had already grown substantially since their wedding a year ago, peppering his face with blonde. The straw hat he wore covered his sandy blonde curls, shadowing his usually cheerful eyes against the sun. He had gotten paler and thinner this summer, changes that Emma attributed to his long hours at the Williams' farm, an Englisch establishment down the road. She knew Eli felt anxious to build his own barn, one they could share, raised and ready to provide enough income to get by, but even with generous donations from the community, they could only afford the small farmhouse they inhabited together.

He sensed her looking at him; he had a way of doing that, after all these months. Their eyes met, for a moment, but she couldn't quite decipher whether his look was one of concern or just weariness. Not for the first time, she felt glad that *Gott* had not decided to bless them with children yet; with so many changes in her and Eli's lives, as she got used to being his wife and he grew familiar with working harder to support them both, she didn't feel ready to be a mother.

Despite the hardships they currently faced, Emma knew she loved her husband. She knew him better than anyone else did. The way he ate the food she cooked, how he enjoyed helping her with the garden at the house; every detail of his life was hers to know, and she felt blessed to have married him.

"Bishop Amos is going to make an announcement!" Martha, Emma's younger sister, had approached the two women, a smile bringing light to her face.

"*Ja*?" Sarah asked, frowning. "I haven't heard rumor of any marriages coming about, have you?"

Martha looked like she wanted to burst from excitement. Emma smiled at her sister, who had recently entered her *rumspringa*, a time before pledging herself to the Church through baptism. Although fickle-headed at times, exploring her new rites as a teenager, Martha still possessed the childlike innocence she had always shown.

"I think this one knows what the announcement will be," she said to Sarah, who grinned as well.

Martha began to speak almost immediately, her voice lowered in a confidential tone. "Mamm says—"

Trust in the LORD with all your heart and lean not on your own understanding; in all your ways acknowledge him, and he will make your paths straight. - Proverbs 56:3

"I worry so about Martha," Emma told Eli that night, after the big picnic. "I just hope Mamm and Daed keep an eye on her, especially with that new telephone."

"With the way your Daed was opposing Bishop Amos before the public announcement, I wouldn't be surprised if Martha never steps foot in that corner of the barn," Eli said, looking up from his carving to smile at her. "A community phone. I've never seen him so angry."

Emma put her towel down, finishing off cleaning the stove. She walked over to where Eli sat, forming a small carving in his hands.

"Daed loves his ways, and adding a community telephone on his land is certainly trying his patience," she agreed, wiping her hands on her apron. "It's a shame it has to be on his farm."

"*Ja*, but it's the cheapest place for the telephone company to build a line out *daar*," Eli replied, with a shrug. "*Gott's* will," he added, solemnly.

She couldn't argue with him, and didn't want to. The carving in his hand was beginning to take shape. She put a hand on his arm, and he paused, looking deep into her eyes. She couldn't help but to notice that his own eyes had dark lines of tiredness beneath them.

"*Je goed voelt*?" she asked him, concerned.

"*Ja*, wonderful-good," he said, and though he gave her a reassuring smile, she didn't feel convinced. She had never seen him look so tired, so weak, before.

"What are you carving?" she asked, wanting to change the subject.

He held up the little carving, made from the wood of a birch tree, with pride. "You know what this is?" he asked her.

She giggled. The carving had two small ears, beady eyes, and a snout. "A pig?" she asked.

He touched the end of her nose with the tip of his finger with a crooked smile. "*Ja*. A pig for our new barn, hm?"

She had to smile. Leaning close, she kissed him on the cheek, feeling the scratch of his unshaven hair against her lips.

"We'll get our barn, Eli," she whispered to him, later that night, listening to his heavy breathing as he slept. "If it's part of *Gott's* plan, we'll have a barn filled with cows, and pigs, and anything you want. Then you'll be home with me, and the children, *Gott*-willing. No more *Englisch* farms for you."

Honor your father and your mother, that your days may be long in the land that the Lord your God is giving you - Exodus 20:12

Aunt Lizzie and Daed had already decried the phone as the work of the devil, but that didn't stop families from the eighteen Amish houses in the area from coming to see the new commodity, placed in an once-inconspicuous corner of Daed and Mamm's barn.

At first, young people trailed through the barn, marveling at the shiny new buttons of the phone, at its pure white cord, at how clear you could hear the beeps and voicemail through the receiver. Not surprisingly, many teenagers in their *rumspringa* already had numbers of some of their *Englisch* friends, and wasted no time calling them for the first time. During the second week of the phone's arrival, older community members came by to speak with Mamm and Daed, and by happenstance they all somehow made their way to the barn, stumbling into the strange *Englisch* object.

Mamm, not as stringent about the phone as Aunt Lizzie and Daed, hadn't found a use for the phone yet, but revealed to Emma after church the second week that the constant parades of people it brought had started to wear on her. She secretly hoped that the fascination would die down, especially since the phone was only to be used for emergency purposes, according to the Bishop.

Martha, in the center of all the attention, remained mostly silent on the subject. According to Sarah, she had been rebuked harshly by Daed when she had asked to use the phone to contact Maria, one of her *Englisch* girlfriends. Since then, Martha's usual teenage sulking had increased tenfold. At one point, she had refused to eat, only convinced by Daed's temper and speeches.

By the third week, the crowds had indeed dispersed, though the phone was still used regularly by some certain individuals, either teenagers or Amish folks who worked for the *Englisch*. Eli never dropped by to see the contraption, preferring to do things as he had always done them; going to work by carriage every day and coming back home by carriage every night. Emma, too, had little interest in the phone, too busy with her devotions and homemaking to have much time to think about it.

It wasn't until a month later, when Eli returned home from the Williamses tired enough to fall asleep at the table, that Emma considered using the phone to call someone. No Amish physician lived near their community, and Eli's condition seemed to be worsening day-by-day, even though he himself wouldn't admit it.

Emma chose another blistering hot afternoon to voice her concerns to Mamm, who always seemed to know the right remedy for everything. With Eli having taken the carriage to work, she was forced to walk nearly two miles to the Bontrager's *hauss*. When she arrived, sweat coated nearly every inch of her body.

"Martha, it is shameful for you to think in such a manner," she could hear Mamm say, as she approached the door. "Sulking around as such isn't going to help solve any problem!"

Emma opened the door, but the conversation between mother and daughter did not end with her entrance. The house's air felt cool against her burning skin, an oasis in the desert.

Martha, who sat in a chair by the window, rocking woefully with her unfinished sewing in her lap, responded to her mother with venom.

"*Nee*, but you and Daed are so unreasonable!" Martha blinked a couple of times, as if seeing Emma for the first time. "Isn't that right, Emma? Remember Jarron Williams? It was only by chance that you talked to him again, and Eric and I will never have that happen!"

Emma remembered riding in the *Englischer* Jarron Williams' big red truck the day that she decided to join the Church. He had been so close to her lips that she could have kissed him, if she had wanted. But she chose Eli, and hadn't looked back.

"Ye will if *Gott* wills it," retorted Mamm before Emma could reply, a slight wry smile touching her lips. "Emma, my sweet! It's been so long since you've come to visit us, come, sit!"

Emma smiled as Mamm embraced her, making sure not to soil her daughter's garments with her hands, stained with cooking grease. Her dark hair was pinned back, exposing red cheeks and her aging face. A dash of flour marked her cheek. Emma wiped it off for her with a thumb.

"Who is Eric?" she asked them both, obeying her mother and sitting down at the table, fingers playing with the folds of her skirt.

Mamm rolled her eyes as Martha launched into a broken, emotional explanation.

"The most wonderful-good *Englisch* boy that ever lived!" she exclaimed, letting her sewing clatter to the floor as she stood up, hands clenched dramatically to her heart. "We met at the cafe, near town! He told me he wants to meet again — I just need to call..."

"Martha Bontrager, enough!" Mamm said, a harsh edge entering her voice. "You will not be using that phone for any such calls! It is for emergency, only!"

"But Sadie uses it for her beau..."

"Sadie should not be having any *Englischer* beau," Mamm interrupted.

Martha fell silent, tears glistening in her eyes, casting an angry glance at Emma, who had said nothing in her defense.

"Mamm is right," Emma said to her, "*Englisch* boys will bring you nothing but trouble, Martha."

"You only say that because you are married already!" Martha said, wiping her eyes with her apron and sitting back down with a huff.

Although she felt sympathy for her sister, knowing the longing to join the *Englisch* world that she herself had experienced at a young age, Emma could say nothing more to bring her peace. Her worry for her husband felt more important than anything in the world at that moment.

"Mamm," she said, watching as Mamm laid out a crust for a pot pie, "I'm worried about Eli."

"*Ach*, a wife worried about her husband?" Mamm said, turning toward her with a wink. "It can't be so! *Wat is het*?"

Emma laid out her troubles for Mamm, starting with Eli's determination to raise a barn of their own, and ending with his sickness. Mamm thought for a moment.

"I would say he's overworked," she finally said with a shrug of her shoulders. "A man like that will work himself to death if you let him. You mustn't let him, Emma. He's got to let things happen in *Gott's* own good time."

Although Mamm's advice came from experience, Emma didn't feel convinced that she was completely right, especially after Eli came home that evening, sweating, tired, but smiling nonetheless.

And without faith it is impossible to please him, for whoever would draw near to God must believe that he exists and that he rewards those who seek him. - Hebrews 11:6

Martha Bontrager had run away, they said. Ran away with an *Englisch* boy. No one knew for sure if she'd come back.

"She'll come back," Sarah said, rocking little Isaac so furiously Emma thought they might both fall off the chair. "She has to come back."

Daed had gone out looking for Martha, along with Mamm, an exhausted Eli, Sarah's husband Jeremiah, and several other neighbors, Amish and *Englisch*. Bishop Amos had told them to have no fear, to walk in the light though the darkness seemed to surround them, but Emma could not quite find her faith this night. In the dim light of Sarah and Jeremiah's house, everything seemed out of control, unclear. Emma peered out into the darkness through the window, feeling a shiver overcome her body.

"Emma?" Sarah stared at her, eyes pleading, looking for some semblance of hope in Emma's response.

Isaac giggled, tugging on his mother's hair lightly, wanting to play.

"Oh Sarah," Emma breathed, sitting down herself, "Don't ask me questions like that. All we can do is have faith in the Lord."

"*Ja,*" Sarah said, nodding in agreement, "*Ja,* faith is the only thing we can rely on."

Emma wished she could heed her own advice and stop worrying. Martha, silly Martha; she'd run away with the *Englisch* boy, Eric, and now no one knew where she had gone. Emma wondered if she had visited him in some *Englisch* clothes he had given her, or if she had worn her dress out into the secular world. Did she know what she had gotten herself into? If she had escaped in the boy's vehicle, they would have been long gone by now. The Amish searchers would have no luck, in their slower modes of transportation.

"I simply cannot sit here and wait any longer," she thought aloud, startling Sarah and Isaac, who gurgled. "Sarah, didn't Jeremiah used to work for the Williams family? Do you have the phone number? I know Eli had a business card, but it's at our house."

Sarah thoughts for a moment, getting up and shifting through a few drawers, Isaac balanced on one hip. Isaac stared up at Emma through big, brown eyes. After a few minutes of searching, Sarah produced a crisp, yellowed business card. "WILLIAMS & WILLIAMS FARM EQUIPMENT," it read.

"I'm not sure if this is up to Daede —" Sarah began, but Emma had already snatched the card from her hand.

Outside, the air had cooled. Crickets chirped, oblivious to the trouble above them. Emma began to jog, thinking only of the phone in Daed and Mamm's barn. Her heart began to beat hard against her chest as she lengthened her strides, glad that at least Sarah's house was decently close to the barn.

With numb fingers, she picked up the receiver of the phone. She had used one once, to call for someone to pick her up from the supermarket when her ride accidentally left without her. She dialed the number on the business card, doubting that anyone would be in at this time of night.

"Hel...Hello?" A groggy voice picked up on the fourth ring, just as Emma had been ready to give up.

She knew the voice. Her body went rigid as memories flooded through her, as the image of a young man with auburn hair filled her mind.

"Hello?" the voice asked again.

"Jarron," she said. "This is Emma, Emma Bontrager...Yoder."

"Emma?" the voice sounded less groggy. "You have a phone? What's..."

"It's for emergencies," she said, her voice higher-pitched than she had intended. "Jarron, it's my sister Martha. She's in trouble. I need... I need..." Tears pooled in her eyes.

For nothing is hidden that will not be made manifest, nor is anything secret that will not be known and come to light - Luke 8:17

The red truck pulled into view twenty minutes after they had hung up. Jarron Williams looked much the same as last year, though he had a few streaks of auburn on his recently unshaven face. A green John Deere cap covered his hair, though some of it had made its way out of the material.

Jarron suggested checking at the cafe in town before anything. Emma, shamed to have been so panicked on the phone, simply nodded.

"How have you been, Em?"

He had never used a nickname for her before, and she wasn't sure she liked it. "Wonderful-good," she replied, staring out the window, as if by some gift of *Gott* Martha would be outside, waving to her.

"Eli says you've adapted to married life pretty well," Jarron said, glancing over at her. He and Eli worked together on the Williams farm, and Emma knew that Eli respected Jarron very much, but she hadn't expected her husband to gossip about her. "Says you worry about him too much, though," he added, emitting a strained laugh.

Emma frowned at the statement. Eli's condition had not improved, and despite her best efforts, she could not get him to take work off. On top of his constant weariness, his appetite had gotten worse, and he had probably lost another ten pounds. Although he had always been thin, his eyes now sat deep in their sockets, muscles giving way to bone. She felt afraid of losing him, of him fading away.

"I do worry about him," she admitted. "I'm afraid he's overworking himself. He wants to raise a barn for us; we're so close, and he doesn't want to stop now."

"Yeah, I agree that he's overworking himself, especially with his condition," Jarron said. Emma grew cold as he continued, oblivious to her reaction. "When we had to take him into the doctor..."

"The doctor? An *Englisch* doctor?" Emma tried to move her fingers. They felt frozen, immobile.

Jarron stopped speaking, looking over at her, confused. "Yeah. The day he passed out while working the crane...you...you knew about that, right?"

"Jarron," she said, swallowing hard. "Jarron, you must tell me everything."

Jarron hesitated, and, as if *Gott* had willed it, his cellphone buzzed in his pocket. Emma tried to breathe, even though it felt like someone sat on her chest, forcing the air from her lungs.

"Oh, thank God," Jarron said into the phone. "Sure, thanks Dad." He hung up, slouching in his seat. He turned toward her, smiling. "Dad and the crew found your sister. She was at the train station about five miles out of town. They caught her before she could get away. They are driving her home now."

"You had your *Daed* go and look?" Emma asked, mortified at waking the whole *Englisch* community over her sister's foolish nature.

Jarron shrugged. "Us country folk like to help out the neighbors."

Despite the good news, and despite the fact that she could breathe a little easier, Emma still felt immobile, sinking into the seat of Jarron's truck.

"Jarron."

He turned his gaze back toward the road, which looked deserted save for the dim headlights of his truck. "Emma, if Eli didn't want you to know..."

"He didn't," she said, staring out the front of the truck, into the dark unknown. "But you'll tell me everything."

Book Three: The Englischer's Gift

"Watch and pray that you may not enter into temptation. The spirit indeed is willing, but the flesh is weak." - Matthew 26:41

When Emma Yoder saw the big red truck pull up into the drive of Miller's Amish Furniture Store, her chest tightened. She stood up from the chair she had seated herself on, adjusting Isaac on her hip. He gurgled with delight.

"Have a wonderful-good day," Emma's sister, Sarah, said from where she stood in front of the register. She gave their newest customers, two English women who wore fur coats and had nails that shone red as freshly-picked apples, their change.

Ever since Sarah and her husband, Jeremiah Miller, had founded the store just six months ago, Emma had witnessed a change in her once reserved, conservative sister. She had taken to wearing her hair down in an English fashion, though she still wore her Plain clothing, and she smiled more easily. Their *mamm* had noticed, and had commented on the changes on more than one occasion, but Emma had no judgment to pass on her older sister, especially when her own life had embraced English influences in more than one, dangerous way.

One such influence walked into the store a moment later, letting in a cool breeze of winter air. The *Englischer* Jarron Williams, co-owner of the Williams and Williams Farm Equipment, met her eyes. The look on his face told her all she needed to know.

The English ladies exited the building, brushing past him on their way out. He found his way to the counter in seconds.

"I'm coming," Emma said stiffly, before he could speak. "Sarah — here, take Isaac."

Sarah took her son without paying him any attention. Her eyes went from Jarron to Emma, then back again.

"*Hallo,* Mr. Williams, it is nice to see you again," she said, and Emma could see tears glistening in her eyes.

Jarron nodded, the corners of his mouth only slightly curving with some semblance of a smile. Emma donned her coat and winter bonnet, shrugging into the old material. She had noticed dozens of places where her coat needed mending, what seemed like hundreds of loose threads threatened to dissolve the coat altogether, but her life — her new job at the store, her duties as a wife to Eli, and his condition — felt too hectic to think too long about much of anything.

"Send my love to our Eli," Sarah whispered to her, hugging her tight. Emma could hear the slight shake in her sister's voice, but she herself had no more tears to spare.

"Come to me, all who labor and are heavy laden, and I will give you rest. Take my yoke upon you, and learn from me, for I am gentle and lowly in heart, and you will find rest for your souls." - Matthew 11:28-29

"You look thinner, Em," Jarron said as they bumped along the old country road.

Emma didn't answer. She stared out the window, into the light sheen of dirty snow covering the fields. Spring would be here soon, cleaning off the brown slush to make way for flowers and budding trees. She knew she shouldn't be so rude to Jarron, who had been helping her and Eli for the last year — making appointments, giving them rides, taking it easy on Eli's work schedule — but her tongue couldn't seem to form the words she wanted to say. Her thoughts felt blue, foreign to her. The place in her heart reserved for *Gott* had begun to feel empty, void of all life.

Emma had never before experienced such emptiness. When she had found the blood on her skirts, signalling her first miscarriage eight months ago, she had always felt comforted by the fact that it was God's Will, and that he would provide another child for her and Eli. When her little sister, Martha, had ran away with an English boy for the second time and was successful, Emma had felt God's Presence within her, and it had calmed her and filled the place where Martha's charm and wit had once resided. When Eli had begun seeing the English doctor for his condition, what the English physician called "dilated cardiomyopathy," a heart condition that could easily be fatal, Emma had felt afraid but reassured that God's Love was still within her, keeping her alive and well.

Even with the constant support of her friends and family, and Jarron and his father's kindness toward her and her husband, Emma had finally begun to lose hope. Coming home to Eli's tired frame and trying her best to get him to eat had become a ritual; attempting to convince him to stay home rather than working at the Williams' farm had always been a hopeless cause.

She felt a warm pressure on her hand, and looked down to find Jarron's calloused fingers wrapping around hers, the pad of his thumb ever so slightly rolling over her knuckles. This human contact brought the tears she thought she had lost back to her eyes, and she looked back out the window, watching the trees whiz by. At one point in her life, his attention would have made her blush with embarrassment, filling her with guilt and shame.

Now, though, any form of physical contact, no matter how slight, felt right.

"He still wants that barn," she said, quietly, her soft voice pervading the silent cab.

Eli's dream, having a barn of their own, had slipped further and further away from them as the medical bills had piled up.

"I know," Jarron said, hesitating for a moment before continuing. "Emma, I don't think it's about the barn. Dad and I have offered to cover its expenses. He won't take our money."

"*Niet*, he won't take *Englishers'* money," Emma explained. "We already feel so indebted to you, Jarron. We cannot accept any more help. Eli will work himself to death," she said, feeling a chill. Her *Mamm* had told her not to let Eli work himself to death, meaning it as a figure of speech, but Emma thought she might have meant it literally, now.

Jarron snorted, shaking his head, showing what he thought of their philosophy. His hand didn't leave hers, though, and today she felt more grateful than ever for his consideration.

"Count it all joy, my brothers, when you meet trials of various kinds," James 1:2

When they brought Eli back from the doctor's appointment, Jarron had to help him from the truck. Emma opened the door for the two men; Jarron's strong, tall frame supported her husband's weaker, shorter frame as they strode through the door, heading straight for the small bedroom in the corner of their modest home.

"Who are you?" she heard Eli ask.

Emma nearly jumped out of her skin as she turned to find a dead English woman sitting at her kitchen table, head at an awkward angle, eyes closed. Emma's hands flew to her mouth, covering it as she examined the intruder. Upon further inspection, she realized the woman was not in fact dead, but had fallen asleep where she sat.

The woman had layered purple-red hair that had drawn down in front of her face in sleep. Through the strands Emma could see the face of a thin young girl with unnaturally pale skin and fake red cheeks.

"What the — " Jarron began, and suddenly the girl jolted awake, hands pushing back her hair as she looked around wildly.

"Where am..." Her voice was high-pitched, frightened. "Where am I? Oh!"

Eli cried out as the girl flew over to her, hugging her with a hungry ferocity. Emma, startled, looked at Jarron and her husband, who looked just as bewildered as she felt.

"Emma! Emma, sweet sister! It's me!"

The girl looked up from the embrace, wiping the hair out of her face to reveal black-rimmed eyes with unnaturally long eyelashes. Emma suddenly noticed the eyes themselves, and managed a breath before a smile overcame her face.

"Martha!"

Her little sister beamed at the recognition, hugging her sister tightly as Emma's arms began to wrap around her.

"Where have you been, little one?" Eli wheezed, letting Jarron sit him down in the chair where Martha had sat.

Emma looked at her husband from over Martha's skinny shoulder. He leaned heavily on the wooden table, slumping over as his blue eyes took in the scene. His face, covered in his ever-growing beard, looked gaunt, almost unrecognizable, but the smile that touched his lips was his and his alone. She knew he smiled from the joy Martha had given her; he had told her once that his heart beat for hers. Why, then, had that beat go faulty?

Martha drew away from Emma, keeping hold of her hand as she turned toward Eli.

"Vegas, baby, Vegas!" she said in a way that made Emma think that her words were an English euphemism, though she herself had never heard it. "And you, brother-in-law of mine! When'd you get so thin?"

Eli laughed along with her, but Jarron and Emma exchanged a glance with each other as the younger girl hugged Eli fondly. To Emma it seemed like just yesterday when she, Martha, and Eli had walked to

Emile Smith's house, laughing and throwing snowballs. Eli had been so full of life, then. The man who sat at the kitchen table now was only a shell of the man she had known, physically at least. The thought made her mind go numb, so she tried to stop thinking.

"Jarron Williams, how are you?" Martha said, shaking Jarron's hand with confidence. "Didn't think you'd be hanging around here with my sister after all this time," she said, and this time Emma *did* blush.

"Well after we found you the first time you ran away I thought I'd better keep close to see that it didn't happen again," Jarron retorted, and Emma noticed that he didn't smile as widely as he usually did when he spoke to people he knew. "I guess my efforts didn't work too well."

If she sensed the tone of the comment, Martha didn't show it. Her happiness seemed to catch on like wildfire, as Eli smiled as he hadn't done in weeks.

"Do you like my hair?" Martha asked, doing a little twirl as she shook out her uneven hair.

"It's very different," Eli volunteered, earning a giggle and a kiss on the cheek from Martha.

"Have you seen Mamm and Daed yet?" Emma asked, finding Jarron's coldness to be more to her liking.

After weeks of searching and months of heartbreak, it seemed unfitting for her sister to be so happy around the people she had deceived, without any word or correspondence since. Although she had always admired how easy-going and forgiving Eli was, Emma found it hard to be that way herself, even now. Whenever she had imagined her sister coming home, she had imagined her reconciled with the faith, ready to join the Church and live out the journey of the Plain lifestyle. Martha's behavior, however, suggested the opposite; she seemed perfectly content with where she was.

"Not yet," Martha said, volunteering no more information on the subject. "What are you three doing together, anyway?"

"For the anger of man does not produce the righteousness of God." : James 1:20

Late that night, as the wind slipped through the miniscule cracks of their wood home, Emma woke with a start. She sat up, rubbing her eyes as they adjusted to the darkness of their bedroom, lit only by the faint glow of moonlight from outside.

She had dreamt of Eli, of Jarron, perhaps a combination of the two. Whoever it was, this strange Amish man who wore a baseball cap like Jarron was wont to do, had fallen from a tree and laid broken on the ground. He had cried out to her, fingers reaching toward the bottom of her skirts, pain causes his face to contort. The face's features, practically indistinguishable to begin with, twisted until the face itself no longer existed, until only emptiness filled the void...

Emma slid out of bed, bending down to give Eli a kiss on the back of his neck. Her husband stirred a little, but remained sleeping as she exited the room.

"Emma?" she heard a small voice, near the window, say.

Martha had a pair of plaid pajama bottoms and a sweatshirt on. In the din, Emma could see the shimmer of tears on her cheeks. Her blue eyes were more prominent, now that she had removed the dark black makeup. Even despite her unnatural hair color and English clothing, Emma knew the girl as her sister, a woman who up until a year ago had been innocent, healthy, and dedicated to the Church.

Emma felt as if she knew *this* woman, even though the Martha now looked so different.

"*Jah*," she said, closing the door to her bedroom behind her. "Why aren't you asleep?"

Martha looked down at the pile of blankets they had laid out for her, her makeshift bed. She sniffed, wiping her nose with the back of her hand.

"Something's very wrong with Eli, isn't it?" she asked, staring up at Emma, the moonlight reflecting off her blue irises eerily. "You all speak of this heart condition like it's nothing — but it's bad."

Emma felt a surge of anger swell up in her. She clenched a fist, willing herself not to say something she'd regret.

"*Jah*," she replied, simply.

"Aren't you scared?"

"*Nee*, *Gott* will provide," Emma replied, although the words felt foreign, unnatural.

Martha stared at her for a moment more before sighing, staring out the window into the dark gloom. "You've changed, Emma."

"Not as much as you have, sister," she said.

"You're angry? I don't blame you..."

"Don't blame me?" Emma couldn't help but sound harsh. "*You* ran away, Martha, and didn't tell anyone where you were going or if you were going to be back. Now you come back here, acting as if nothing has changed? Look at yourself, look how you've changed! How could you give up your family, your life like that?"

She could see Martha's shoulders shaking with emotion, but Emma continued, unaffected.

"Do you even know how you broke Mam's and Dat's hearts? Look at Eli, look at him — how can you possibly know what he's going through, what he's been through? And me, and Sarah, we've had our own heartbreak, our own sadness — " Emma paused, pressing on her empty belly with her fingertips, remembering how much light the prospect of a baby had brought to Eli's worn face. "*Ach*, and now you come back here, expecting the world from us, expecting us to accept you back..."

"*Nee*," Martha interrupted, turning back toward Emma, a fire coming into her eyes that Emma had never seen before. "No, Emma. I'm not here to come back. I'm here to say goodbye." She lifted her hand. A small ring glittered on her left hand.

"You're getting married?" Emma asked.

Martha nodded. "I wanted to say one last goodbye before we moved. We're going to New York."

Emma felt like a fool. She had known it would be hard to forgive her sister if she had wanted to come back and join the Church after her year of absence, but Martha had, as usual, foiled her expectations.

"You will tell Mamm and Daed about this, *Jah*?"

Martha looked down at her hands, shrugging. "I don't know, Emma. I only have a couple of days, and — I want so much for them to accept me, to accept my choice, but I know it will be so hard for them... "

Emma couldn't find the words to express what she felt. She bade Martha a goodnight, and went to sleep, her back against Eli's.

"A man's gift makes room for him and brings him before the great." Proverbs 18:16

When Jarron Williams and the local preacher, Amos Leander, knocked on the door of the Yoder's home, Eli had fallen back asleep in the bedroom as Emma baked a store-bought chicken potpie, too tired to labor through making anything else for herself to eat. With Eli not eating very much or very often, she had begun to resort to English food to curb her own appetite, not wanting to make him nauseous with the smells of a home-cooked meal.

The two men greeted her kindly, kissing her on the cheek as she invited them in. She felt a pang of remorse that Martha had gone out to say goodbye to her old friends, for she thought the preacher's influence might have convinced her to reconsider her decision, but the bleak nothingness that had overcome her mind and heart prevented her from feeling too much of any one emotion. She had wanted, badly, to tell Sarah about Martha's reappearance, but Eli had told her not to say anything to the rest of her family.

"She'll do it in her own time, beloved," he had told her, smiling despite his pain. "Have faith."

Emma had fallen short on faith lately, and she found it hard to believe him, but she obeyed.

"Eli is asleep," she told Jarron and the preacher, who had sat themselves down on the table. She might have offered them a cup of hot chocolate, or something, but she didn't think she had the energy to heat something up.

"Good," Jarron said, placing his hands flat on the table, leaning over confidentially.

Emma sat down across from them, folding her own hands in her lap. "Good?"

"*Jah*," Amos said, rubbing his beard. He wore dark clothing to cover his long, skinny limbs as usual, but his brown eyes lit with secret excitement as he spoke. "Mr. Williams and I have been discussing something that I'd think you'd like to hear, Emma. He and his father have agreed to help us raise a barn for you and Eli, something that could be completed by spring, if you wanted."

Emma looked back toward the bedroom, but Eli had not stirred. She turned back around the face the men.

"A barn for Eli? But..."

"The community has agreed to pitch in," Jarron said, "And my dad and I have the equipment. You don't need to worry about the money. Think of it as a loan — we lend you the money and materials now, and then once Eli's back on his feet..."

"What if Eli never gets back on his feet?" she blurted, numb to their reactions.

"We must *heb vertrouwen*, have faith, child," Amos said to her, but she stood up, shaking her head.

"Eli wouldn't want this," she said, shaking her head again, feeling pressure build behind her eyes, "No, no, you can't do this," she pleaded, taking in Jarron's gaze, wishing he could understand, "We want to do this by ourselves..."

"It might not be possible to do it by yourselves," Jarron said, his voice quiet. "You just said as much yourself, Emma."

"No!" she said, a sob emitting from her throat. "No, I won't have it! Eli won't have it!"

"Child..." Amos began, but she brushed past him, flying out the door and leaving them behind.

Outside, a light snow was falling, and snowflakes landed on her lightly-clad shoulders, making her shiver. Tears clouded her vision.

She wouldn't think of losing Eli, she couldn't. Someone who she had shared her heart, her mind, and her soul with. Yet the cloud of hopelessness that had descended upon her couldn't be lifted, weighing down her thoughts and preventing her from doing anything, anything at all. Her connection with serenity, with the Gott she had pledged her life to, had disappeared, leaving her empty and cold.

Warmth embraced her suddenly, and she realized that Jarron was holding her, his strong arms cradling her to his chest. Her face buried itself in his jacket as she cried, really cried, for the first time since Eli's diagnosis.

"It'll be okay," he whispered to her, but even she could hear the break in his voice at the thought of his friend, their friend, being anything but well. "I love you, Emma, and I love Eli. He's talked about this barn for months. I know you don't want to accept our help, but we have to do this, for Eli."

"For Eli," she repeated, sniffling. Tears slid down her cheeks. He wiped them away, nodding to her, pleading with her. "A barn for Eli," she said, finally.

THE END

Book Four: Amish Pain

"And if I go and prepare a place for you, I will come again and will take you to myself, that where I am you may be also." John 14:3

Emma cringed as she stepped into a puddle, carrying a bundle of hay toward the barn for the goats. Her shoe and sock were soaked through, making her shiver slightly. The cool spring breeze permeated through her skirts and tugged on her bonnet, making her colder. Although spring was in full swing, with the sun shining up ahead, remnants of the winter clung stubbornly to the land.

She walked toward the barn, standing to the west of their modest home. It was a beautiful thing, made of perfect manufactured Englischer wood delivered with the kindness of the Williams family, and then raised with the help of the Amish community. She might have felt guilty to look at it, since she had reluctantly accepted the help of the Englischers a little over a year ago for her husband's sake, but instead she saw it as the product of the work of a community, both Englisch and Amish, and that within itself made it a beautiful thing. Her *Daed*, ever the conservative one, didn't agree.

"If Gott had wanted us to use the Englisch ways, *dochter*," he had said, "He would have made us Englisch."

Even if he didn't agree, she couldn't help but to feel the barn was a miracle come true. Even the Bishop had pitched in, working side-by-side with the Williams family and their crew. Her husband, Eli, had helped as much as he could, which on that day basically meant offering moral support to everyone and thanking them a thousand times before the project was through.

Once the barn had been raised, proud and strong, he had got down on his knees and cried. She had hardly ever seen Eli cry as much as he did that day, even after being married to him for two and a half years. Jarron Williams, the Englischer who Eli most respected, had hugged him tight.

Even Martha, her younger sister, had agreed to stay for the barn raising.

"It is a beautiful sight," Sarah said, tugging along a bale of hay as she followed Emma up the hill to the barn.

Emma smiled gratefully at her elder sister. Throughout everything, Sarah had always been there for her. Even though Sarah had a child of her own—and another one on the way, from the way she had started talking—she continuously made sure that Emma and Eli were contented, that Emma wasn't being overworked because of Eli's illness. Of all the people in her life, she looked up to Sarah the most. Running a household, owning part of an Amish store, Sarah's life exemplified so many plain virtues, and her faith never seemed to dwindle like Emma's own constantly did.

"I'm so glad Eli got his dream," Sarah said with a smile. "He worked so hard for it. We all did."

The slight smile that had formed on Emma's face vanished as she thought about that instance, a little under a year ago. After that time, everything seemed to have changed. Martha had left with her Englisch fiancé, as Mam and Daed watched in despair. Although she wouldn't be shunned, since she hadn't ever pledged herself to the Church, it would be hard for Martha to come back and visit now without it being extremely awkward. Emma liked to think of Martha the way she had been, when Eli was strong and able and always teasing her about her ink-black hair. Last time she had seen her, her sister's hair had been chopped off and dyed red and purple. Jarron Williams, too, had seemed to vanish. For some reason, she felt pain at his departure. Although she knew from rumors at her sister Sarah's store that he was still in town, word on the street was that he had a new girlfriend, an Englisch one.

Sometimes she felt jealous of them both, Martha and Jarron. Martha for being able to walk away from the community so easily and Jarron for never actually being part of it. She loved the Amish ways and the culture she had grown up in, but being around Eli had begun to take a toll on her. Eli hadn't risen from bed in over a week. Spring had made way for summer, summer changed into fall, fall into winter, and now, a year since his diagnosis of what the Englisch doctor called cardiomyopathy, Eli had finally been grounded. He hated not being able to work. Although he had received his very own barn from the kindness of the Englisch Williams family and the Amish community, he could never be happy as his wife tended to it, doing the jobs that he, as the man of the family, should have been able to do.

He had grown distant from her, lately. She gave him everything he wanted, and more, but nothing seemed to be enough. He would lie in bed day after day, looking out the small window of their bedroom. He had become so thin that sometimes she would lie awake at night, back pressed up against him, just trying to make sure he was still breathing.

She felt as if she lived with a dead man.

"What's wrong, Emma?" Sarah asked as they reached the barn, opening the door and holding it for her.

Emma shook her head, entering the dark building, spreading the hay out for the goats, who bleated their welcome. "Thinking too much," she answered, blinking away tears in her eyes.

Sarah stayed mercifully silent for a few moments, following her and spreading the hay out for the animals.

"Have you heard the big news, yet?" she asked suddenly, clearly trying to cheer her sister up. "Remember Jarron Williams? Sounds like he's going to get married this summer."

Emma felt a sharp pang in her stomach. She couldn't understand why she felt so disappointed at hearing the news. She had always liked Jarron, at least as a friend. Perhaps she missed the time of her own wedding, when everything had been so simple. She wouldn't admit that it was jealousy, ever. She loved Eli with all her heart. Why should she care if an Englischer got married and who he got married to? She thought perhaps it was because she felt that as his friend, she should have been the first to know. But Jarron had avoided her and Eli for months now.

She faked her best smile. "Is that so?"

Sarah nodded. They walked out of the barn together. "She's from California, I've heard."

"So far away!" Emma said, her mind only half on the news. As they headed closer to the house, her thoughts had turned to Eli. Was he watching them through the window right now, wishing he could walk alongside them? Again tears filled her eyes, and she blinked them away.

"*Ja*, and they've only courted for a few months," Sarah shrugged. "Jarron Williams is a good man. I hope he finds happiness with her."

"Me too," Emma replied. She wasn't sure if she meant her words.

"For God so loved the world, that he gave his only Son, that whoever believes in him should not perish but have eternal life." John 3:16

The next week, news of the Williams wedding had spread to the entire community. As one of the more involved Englischers in the Amish community, Jarron Williams was something of a celebrity among them, a favorite among the inevitable gossip after Church, especially among the women.

Emma didn't hear much of it. Eli had ended up in the Englisch hospital, again, this time with what looked like pneumonia. She sat by his bedside day after day, hitching rides with the Englischers who volunteered to transport Amish people to and from stores and such for their needs.

"*Het spijt me*, my sweet," Eli said to her one night. She could hear the beep of his heart monitor to her right. She sat in the corner of the room, surrounded by shadows, and leaned closer to him, pulling her chair up to his bedside. Sarah's husband, Jeremiah, slept in the other corner of the room, snoring softly. He was as wonderful-good as Sarah was, having agreed to accompany Emma on nighttime vigil. "I haven't been a good husband to you," he continued, voice breaking a little, barely above a whisper.

"That's not true," Emma protested, stopping as he took her hand in his.

"Emma, I feel that Gott is calling to me," he said.

No, not yet, she thought. She had been trying to pray for the last couple of hours, trying to reason with the invisible substance that was Gott. She could remember a time when his light and heat and filled her heart and soul, but that flame had seemed to have extinguished. Nothing felt clear, or certain. She had prayed for strength, for courage, for Eli. Had Gott simply disregarded her prayers completely?

"That's not true, either," Emma said, squeezing his hand.

A tear slid down his cheek, and Emma wiped it away with her thumb, pressing her check up against his scruffy beard. He smelled different. She had become used to smelling his sweat and a healthy amount of dirt after a long day's work. Now he smelled sterile, like the Englisch cleaning supplies.

"I don't want to leave you," he admitted, and she could feel his fingers twitch as he tried to squeeze her hand with all the strength he could muster. His fingers, once calloused and strong from working at the Williams farm, now felt soft and thin. "I don't think Gott is going to give me a choice, though, my dear wife."

"Don't speak in such ways," she told him, brushing his hair across his forehead soothingly. "The Englisch doctors will make you better, and you and I will go home and work in the barn together."

"No, Emma," he said, reaching up to touch her cheek lightly. "I'm sorry. It is not in Gott's Will that I should stay with you."

Emma felt the heat of anger rise from her chest into her head. How could Gott take away Eli from her? Where would she go, after he was gone? Did he truly hear Gott in his head, or was that the medication they had given him?

"Emma," he whispered, blue eyes searching hers. "You must be strong, like always. Live for Gott. He will provide..."

"No!" she cried, hugging him tight, feeling his rib cage against her fingers. "No, you can't leave me, Eli!" she begged now, pleading with him, willing him to live.

She had never lost someone so close to her, except when her *Daed*'s *mamm* had died a few years ago. But she recognized the look in Eli's eyes; he was ready.

"I don't want you to be here," Eli said, not unkindly. "I cannot die with you watching, Emma. Please."

"I can't leave you," she said, tears rolling down her face now. "You can't leave me. You can't."

"Go," he told her, kissing her lightly on the forehead as she leaned down toward him. His lips felt cold. "Go, my wife. My wonderful-good woman. You have a beautiful heart. Share it with the world. Jeremiah," he called, waking the man up. "Take Emma home."

"No!" she cried, holding him more tightly. "You can't do this to me, Eli! You must live!"

He took a deep, laborious breath.

"Jesus said to her, "I am the resurrection and the life. Whoever believes in me, though he die, yet shall he live," John 11:25

She knew she dreamed, because Martha stood in front of her, with black hair that had never been cut. Eli stood there, too, smiling at Emma, grabbing her hand and giving her a twirl. Sarah and Jeremiah, taking turns holding their little son Isaac, spoke with the Bishop underneath the big maple by Aunt Lizzie's house. Sarah had grown large with child. Mamm and Daed sat together near the maple tree with their relatives, uncharacteristically showing affection in public with each other, enjoying their daughters' company.

Emma heard herself laugh as Eli caught her after the spin, hugging her tightly, stroking her hair. He kissed her forehead with warm, full lips. She had never felt happier, not even on her wedding day. Everyone smiled and laughed, kicking off their shoes and dancing with joy, the way she used to see people do in Englisch movies during her *rumspringa*, her running around time. They rejoiced in the beauty of their surroundings, in the company of each other. Suddenly everyone joined hands and spun, around and around, in a big circle, giggling and singing their praises to Gott and his good will.

Jarron approached from outside the circle. He met Emma's eyes, and his look faded the joy in her heart.

"Emma," he said, "Wake up..."

She squeezed Eli's hand a little tighter and turned away from the outsider, trying to find Eli's face to give him a smile.

"Wake up, Emma."

She sat up, looking around in panic for a moment as she tried to discover where she was. Jarron Williams sat on the edge of her bed, taking his hand off her shoulder. She might not have recognized him, after this year of being apart; he'd gotten taller, it seemed, and a little fuller. His auburn stubble had grown into a trimmed beard, covering his face. He wore his characteristic baseball cap; this one had a tractor on the front of it. Whatever look of boyishness he had possessed had long gone. A man sat before her.

"Jarron?" she said, still groggy from her sleep.

"Emma." When he said her name it sounded like a caress. She looked around the room. Out the window, all she could see was darkness; not even the light of the moon showed as it usually did, outlining the barn and all its glory.

"Eli," she said suddenly, her dream fading away, replaced by the harsher reality.

Jarron stopped her from getting up. "You've been sleeping all day, Em," he said, using his special nickname for her.

"Eli," she repeated, the lump in her throat too big to swallow.

His look told her all she needed to know. Eli Yoder, her husband, confidant, and best friend, had left this earth. Her house was still and quiet, void of all life. She was a widow. The thought did more than chill her. Darkness clawed at the edges of her vision. *Lord,* she prayed, *Why?*

"I'm alone," she stated, more for herself than for Jarron.

"Your *mamm* is on her way," Jarron said. "Sarah wanted to come, too, but you told Jeremiah not to let her, remember?"

She could barely remember getting home after seeing Eli, with Jeremiah. She didn't know how Jarron had known to come. She could understand her telling Jeremiah not to let Sarah come; her sister had been more than gracious to her, and she didn't want her to see her in this state.

"Sometimes shock does strange things to your memory," Jarron said, noticing her confusion.

"How did you..." she struggled to find the right words.

Jarron sighed, rubbing his hat back and forth on his head a couple of times before letting it rest where it had been. "Eli called me. From the hospital," he added.

"He..."

"He was worried about you. He wanted you to know that he'll always..." Jarron's voice broke, and he wiped at his eyes angrily. "He was a good friend to me. I didn't do enough for him."

Emma wasn't as composed. She had thought, wrongly, that she had ran out of tears. Jarron scooped her into his arms. The scratchy flannel of his shirt rubbed up against her cheek, but it felt comforting to her.

The door behind Jarron opened. Emma tried to contain her sobs as Mamm walked in, Sarah and—Martha!—trailing behind her. Martha had dyed her hair brown, this time, though it was still cut short. She still looked impossibly thin, and pale, but the tears on her cheeks told Emma that she had heard the news. She didn't know how Martha had known to come; perhaps this was what Jarron had meant when Eli had told him that he would always be there for them all.

"Gott willed it that it be so," Mamm quoted, thought tears sparkled in her own eyes.

Jarron pulled away from her, keeping hold of her left hand, squeezing her fingers tightly. She noticed, not for the first time, how different his hands felt from Eli's. The thought brought more sobs as her family enveloped her in a hug.

"And the dust returns to the earth as it was, and the spirit returns to God who gave it." Ecclesiastes 12:7

A good dozen buggies trailed behind the slow-moving hearse, before they had laid Eli down for his final rest. Cars, too, followed behind the procession, since Eli had made friends with many of the Englischers at the Williams farm where he had worked for much of his life. Emma met everyone with her sisters by her side, even though many of the Amish folk gave Martha strange looks. Martha didn't seem to mind; she had taken the death hard. She had been close to Eli, too.

As the last of the guests left, carrying with them some leftovers from the large lunch they had prepared for the occasion, Emma asked for some time alone with Eli's newly dug grave. They had placed it near his grandfather's, marked with a plain, unadorned gravestone. Emma knew she would never forget it was his, though. She would never forget him, the man who had touched her life, either.

"He was a good man in life, and in death," she heard a voice say behind her. "He was a good friend, too. I wish now I hadn't been so distracted with everything in my world. I'm sorry, Emma."

She turned to find Jarron in his suit, hands in his pockets as he gazed at the grave.

"*Ja,*" she simply replied, "He was at that."

"Thank you for inviting me to come," he said, taking a few steps forward so he stood beside her. They both looked down at the grave.

"You were one of his good friends," she said, nodding. "And you have been more than a help to me. You are welcome in our—my," she corrected herself, willing herself not to think about what those words meant in regard to her widowhood. "My home, anytime. Your fiancée, too. Any friend of yours is a friend of mine."

Jarron gave her smile. "Thanks for that, Em. She's from California, you know, so I can't imagine her coming out here, but it's a kind thought."

He looked down at the ground again, his face growing serious. "If you ever need anything, Emma, you let me know, okay? I won't stay away like I did before."

She nodded, unable to speak. He gave her a hug and walked away, taking slow steps, as if he expected her to say something.

She didn't.

"Goodbye, Eli," she said instead, turning away from the grave and toward where her sisters and family waited.

Book Five: Amish Apology

"For everything there is a season, and a time for every matter under heaven: a time to be born, and a time to die; a time to plant, and a time to pluck up what is planted; a time to kill, and a time to heal; a time to break down, and a time to build up; a time to weep, and a time to laugh; a time to mourn, and a time to dance; a time to cast away stones, and a time to gather stones together; a time to embrace, and a time to refrain from embracing" - Ecclesiastes 3:1-14

The spring breeze shifted, blowing off some of the leaves that had been resting on Eli Yoder's headstone. Emma Bontrager frowned as she bent a little closer, realizing that some of the leaves had left red-orange stains on the unmarked stone. She rubbed at the stains with her hand, only succeeding in smearing them a bit and coating her fingers with dirt.

"Dirt!" her nephew, Isaac, said, crouching down to playfully look at the gravestone. His tiny hand patted the stone as he looked up at Emma. "Dirt!"

"*Ja*, Isaac," Emma replied with a soft smile.

The ground felt cold and hard beneath her as she leaned back from where she sat, looking up at the blue sky. Isaac continued with his rambling; the toddler, still mastering language, never found a moment when he didn't like to exercise his vocal chords.

"It's a beautiful day, Eli," Emma told her late husband. "Can you feel the sun?"

No answer, as usual. She had come to this same place for over a year now and the answer was always the same—nothing. Most times, she felt as if she had died along with Eli in that Englisch hospital bed, struggling to breathe until his heart finally stopped. Her life had certainly stopped.

Often she would look at the barn, Eli's barn, on the hill, once filled with the calls of animals and scents of hay and oats. Now, nothing. She couldn't work at her sister Sarah's store and manage a barn by herself, along with babysitting.

She laughed as Isaac plopped down, grabbing fistfuls of damp leaves that had managed to survive the winter and throwing them up in the air. Even her laugh sounded dead, empty to her ears.

"Leaves," she told Isaac, picking up one herself and throwing it up in the air. He watched as it sunk down, fascinated.

She enjoyed spending time with her young nephew, especially since Sarah was always so busy now with her second child, little Ruthie. Although Emma still owned her house since Dat had agreed to help her out financially, she had taken to spending more time at Sarah and Jeremiah's little homestead, just so she'd be around people.

"Uncle Eli thinks you've grown since the last time you came to visit," Emma told Isaac.

He looked at her a blinked. "Emm-y?"

"*Niet*, Isaac. Uncle Eli."

Isaac thought for a moment then kept playing with the leaves. Perhaps he didn't remember Eli. No one seemed to remember, a lot of the time. Sarah would often look at her and give her a sad smile every time she mentioned him, but others didn't like to talk about him at all.

"Sarah said I'd find you here," a familiar voice rang in her ears. She looked up, shielding her eyes against the sun.

Mamm's greying hair shimmered in the sunlight, casting a pretty glow about her face. Her eyes took in the sight of Emma before turning to gaze upon her grandchild.

"Is something wrong?" Emma asked, worry filling her.

"*Niet*, child," Mamm said, giving her a smile as she bent down, giving Isaac a little tickle. "I thought you might like some company."

She continued playing with Isaac as Emma fell silent. She didn't know where to begin, or even how to talk to anyone anymore.

"Martha sent word," Mamm finally broke the silence, glancing over at Emma. "She said she's coming to visit soon and that her and Eric are doing very well."

"They still have not married, *ja*?" Emma asked, only mildly interested.

She hadn't seen her sister in over a year, and had put her out of her mind. She had once thought a sister's bond was unbreakable, but she now could not bear to hear news of Martha's Englisch life. Martha never bothered to write anyone, usually, except Mamm once in a while. At one time, Emma would have given anything to have heard from her youngest sister, to have known what was going on.

Those days had long passed. Eli was gone, and so was Martha, as far as Emma was concerned. Dat felt similarly, hardly ever speaking to Martha even when she was around.

"Not yet, but they are still engaged," Mamm hastily said, though her voice didn't hold much hope for her daughter ever getting married. Martha had been engaged for years now, and nothing more serious had ever happened.

"I didn't see you during the service on Sunday," Mamm finally said.

Emma dug her hands into the mossy, moist ground. "*Ja,*" she replied, refusing to comment anymore.

It was true that Emma had skipped more than one service. She disliked going anywhere the community was, with their sympathetic whispers and stares. Even more, the place she had reserved in her heart for Gott felt as gone as Eli was. Anger, sadness, perhaps resentment— these emotions had filled its place.

The thoughts of Martha and the Englischer Jarron Williams and her other friends who no longer spoke to her had gone there, too. She had come to believe that friendship never lasted. Martha had left and hardly a word had passed between them since, and Jarron's sudden disappearance in her life came as no surprise after the emotional trauma he'd witnessed around her. He had promised Eli that he would take care of her, be her friend in the face of adversity, but his new marriage must have changed those plans.

"*Wat is er mis?*" Mamm asked, concerned.

"*Niets,*" Emma said, shrugging. "I just haven't been able to go."

Mamm did not push her, and for that Emma was grateful.

"*Ach*, it is a bit chilly out. Come," Mamm said, picking up Isaac.

Emma's eye widened. A huge wet stain showed on the seat of Isaac's little trousers. "Oh, *Mamm!*" Emma exclaimed.

Mamm followed her gaze and her concerned face broke into a huge smile.

"What a big stain for such a little man!" Mamm said, laughing. "We must get you dried off—"

She was interrupted by Emma, who started laughing as she herself stood up. The entire back of her skirt was soaked. Emma began laughing so hard that her stomach began to hurt. She couldn't remember the last time she had laughed like this.

"It seems you both went for a bit of a swim," Mamm said, laughing right along with her daughter. "Eli was always a joker, wasn't he? Looks like he can still fool you."

Emma looked at her mother, tears filling her eyes at the mention of Eli, tears of loneliness but of joy as her laughter continued. Mamm smiled at her, shifting Isaac to one arm while she held out her other hand for Emma.

"There was a rich man who was clothed in purple and fine linen and who feasted sumptuously every day. And at his gate was laid a poor man named Lazarus, covered with sores, who desired to be fed with what fell from the rich man's table. Moreover, even the dogs came and licked his sores. The poor man died and was carried by the angels to Abraham's side. The rich man also died and was buried, and in Hades, being in torment, he lifted up his eyes and saw Abraham far off and Lazarus at his side." Luke 16:19-31

She had promised Mamm that she'd go to the service on Sunday, so she did with Sarah and her family.

Aunt Lizzie was the first to greet her, hugging her so hard that she thought her bones might break. Dat looked at her with a small smile. Mamm enveloped her in a gentle hug, whispering how proud of Emma she was. Other community members made their way over to her before the service began as well, and none of them brought up Eli. This time, she was grateful. She didn't want their sympathy.

As Bishop Amos began to speak, a few late stragglers came in, respectfully standing in the back. Emma glanced over her shoulder as Bishop Amos continued his sermon; she had already lost interest in hearing Gott's Word.

A flash of plaid caught her eye, and she followed it, craning her neck a little.

"What are you looking at?" Sarah asked her in a whisper, balancing a sleeping Ruthie on her arm.

Emma turned a little more and gasped. The Englischer, Jarron Williams, stood in the back of the room. He looked older and a little sadder, but she still recognized him. She could see other surprised looks from the Amish people, most of whom knew either Jarron or his father.

"Jarron Williams is here," Emma told Sarah, leaning in so her voice wouldn't be heard.

"What? *Why?*" Sarah asked excitedly. She liked Jarron, and no one had seen him around in the past couple of months. Emma had seen him on and off during the first year of Eli's death, but Jarron had then just been married and soon his presence in her life and dwindled.

"I don't know."

Emma looked back once more. Jarron listened attentively to bishop Amos, his eyes never straying from the man, even as whispers surrounded him. He no longer wore his characteristic baseball cap, and he had shaved his face. His auburn curls had grown a bit longer, falling across his forehead.

She turned toward the bishop once more, clasping her hands together. What exactly was Jarron Williams doing in an Amish service? Bishop Amos didn't so much as look at Jarron, even though he could probably clearly see him in the back. Perhaps the two men had chatted; Amos was pretty close with Jarron's father, after all.

Emma decided to put it out of her mind. Jarron was hardly even her friend. They had shared a lot while Eli was still alive, but soon after he had died Jarron had gotten married and hardly ever corresponded with her. She didn't particularly feel angry with Jarron, but still refused to see him as anything but an acquaintance of hers. Eli and Jarron had been friends—that didn't mean she and Jarron had to be.

"And without faith it is impossible to please him, for whoever would draw near to God must believe that he exists and that he rewards those who seek him." - Hebrews 11:6

When the service ended, the Amish folk swamped Jarron with questions. Where had he been? How was his wife? How was his father? Their business? No one asked the question that everyone wanted the answer to: Why had he come to a Plain service? Was he thinking of becoming one of them?

As everyone crowded around Jarron, Sarah turned to Emma with a laugh. "I've never quite seen an Englischer who was as welcome in our community as Jarron Williams is."

"*Ja*," Emma said, holding out her hands for Ruthie, who was just now opening her bright blue eyes. Sarah handed her the baby, shaking out her arms.

"He has certainly done more than one good service for our family," Sarah observed as they began to make their way out of the little room. "I'll never forget what he did for Martha when she ran away with that Englisch boy."

Or what he did for Eli, Emma added silently, unwilling to bring those instances up right now. Jarron had always seemed to show up when she needed him most, in times of emergency and struggle. They had been through a lot together with Eli, but now that Eli was dead, Emma was unsure if Jarron still remembered her at all.

Try as she might, she still couldn't forget the first time she had met Jarron, at Emile Smith's house. He had offered to take her for a ride in his big red truck, but Emma had declined. She had chosen Eli over Jarron, thinking she belonged in the Plain community. Jarron had ended up working with Eli, and they had become close friends. The day after Eli's death, he had come into Emma's room, woken her with the tragic news, and held her in his arms as she cried into his shirt.

She felt embarrassed, looking back at those situations now, especially with Jarron in the room right now. She felt the heat rise in her face as she blushed, keeping her head down and tending to the gurgling baby as she slipped past everyone and walked outside. She breathed in the fresh air, trying to stop herself from blushing.

"Emma, it was good to see you today," Bishop Amos greeted her, reaching out to pat her shoulder as he grinned. "And this is baby Ruth, correct?"

"Ja," Emma said shyly. She wasn't used to talking with the bishop. The last time she had spoken with him personally had been during Eli's final few years, about the barn. "Baby Ruthie, we call her."

The preacher's grin widened. "Baby Ruthie. How is her mother doing?"

"Sarah is well, thank you for asking," Emma told him, giving him a small smile back.

"And you, my child? What about you?"

"Wonderful-good," Emma lied. She had always been told lying was a sin, but the penalty to lying to a bishop hadn't been discussed. She wondered briefly what Gott thought of that.

Amos seemed to sense her sadness. Again he patted her on the shoulder, trying to catch her gaze. "I am always here if you ever need to talk, Emma. Please do not hesitate. I know in times of tragedy it seems Gott has disappeared, but..."

"Bishop," Jarron Williams said in greeting, coming up behind Emma. Emma stepped aside, and couldn't help herself from looking up at Jarron, noticing again that he didn't wear his boyish baseball cap anymore. "How are you? Thank you for allowing me to attend today's service."

"Jarron Williams," Amos said, sticking out his hand for a handshake. "It was my pleasure. You remember Emma Bontrager?"

"Yes," Jarron smiled, looking over at her. "Hi, Em."

Em. The nickname sent a small shiver down her spine. He called her that, as if she was some Englisch girl, but he knew she was Plain through and through. It was an endearing term of their old friendship, perhaps.

"*Hallo*," she said, rocking Ruthie.

The bishop excused himself as someone called his name, leaving Emma standing by Jarron. She searched through the crowd, wishing Sarah would come and save her. But Sarah was talking with Aunt Lizzie, who would probably talk her ear off until Sarah could excuse herself away.

"So this is Sarah's new addition?" Jarron asked, grinning at Ruthie, who looked up at him with a toothless giggle.

"*Ja*, Ruthie," Emma said, her tone clipped.

Jarron rubbed the back of his neck. "Is there somewhere we could talk?" he asked her, lowering his voice a little.

"To what end?" Emma retorted. She didn't want to let Jarron in her life again. He had broken her heart when he had suddenly left her life, leaving her alone like Martha had. She didn't want to think about him anymore.

"Please, Emma?" Jarron's eyes searched hers. "You know I wouldn't ask if it wasn't important."

"I will restore to you the years that the swarming locust has eaten, the hopper, the destroyer, and the cutter, my great army, which I sent among you." Joel 2:25

She gave Ruthie to Sarah and she and Jarron walked down the dirt road away from where the community had gathered. Jarron's boots sent little stones from the road flying with every step. He shoved his hands in his pockets, and occasionally she could see him glance at her.

Emma herself kept her eyes on the road, composed.

"Are you angry with me?" Jarron finally asked.

"*Niet*," Emma answered instantly.

"I think you are."

"*Niet*."

"Tell me the truth," he insisted.

She felt him touch her arm, gently grabbing hold of it and stopping her from walking, making her face him. "I am not angry," she said. "I don't know what you want me to say, Jarron."

His green eyes searched hers for a moment. He began to say something, then stopped. "Look, Emma, I know you're Amish. I know anger isn't something that you're supposed to have. But I also know that you're human. You can tell me. I hurt you, didn't I? I already know you're hurt."

"If you already know, why are you asking me?"

"I don't know," he admitted with a sigh.

"Why were you at the service?" she asked, changing the subject.

"I had to see you," he said. She had never quite seen him like this. She had seen him sorrowful, regretful, even grief-stricken. She had never seen him so unsure of himself. "I wanted to tell you personally that I'm sorry. I know I say that every time I go away, but this time, Emma, I swear, I am. I was—afraid, I guess. I wasn't a good friend to you, just like I wasn't a good friend to Eli. I always want to get involved and be there for you, but something always gets in the way."

Tears filled Emma's eyes. He had brought up Eli, and he still remembered her. "Where have you been?" she asked, her voice breaking a little. She shook her head as he went to hug her, not wanting him to hold her again.

"In California," he replied. "My wife wanted to move there so we did—I used it as an excuse to get away from here, away from all the sadness. And—Em, I swear, if I could do it over I would. I left you when you needed me most."

Emma shook her head. She had no right to expect Jarron to be there for her constantly. She knew that, now. Although the hurt she had felt at his going away still hurt, the anger that had filled her heart against him seemed to have dissipated.

"Jarron, you don't have to come back and apologize. You have your own life to lead."

"I want my life to have you in it, Emma Bontrager. I want us to be friends again. I know you're probably still hurting over Eli, still feeling alone. I want to help you, to care for you. Do you think we can do that? Be friends again, I mean?"

"Of course," Emma said, tears filling her eyes at his words once more. She could have sworn all of her tears had already been shed, yet her body seemed to be able to make up new ones all the time.

"Thank you, Emma, for another chance. I swear, I'm not going to take off like I did before. I'm not afraid, anymore."

"Therefore, if anyone is in Christ, he is a new creation. The old has passed away; behold, the new has come." 2 Corinthians 5:17

That afternoon, Emma went down to Eli's grave with Sarah and Baby Ruthie. The sun began to set in the distance, casting an orange glow across their faces. Sarah said nothing as Emma placed a few flowers on his headstone. Although Emma knew Eli was in heaven, she hoped he was looking down at her right now. She tried to smile for him.

Ruthie started to cry as they stood there.

"Het spijt," Sarah muttered, trying to rock the baby back to sleep.

"Niet," Emma said, giving a genuine smile to her sister, face warmed by the sunlight. "It is fine."

As she turned back to the gravestone, her smile widened. For some reason, a sense of peace overcame her mind and soul.

"Thank you, Eli," she said, because she knew it had come from him. At that moment she knew that she could put the past behind her. Not forget it but treasure it, keeping the memories close. But now she knew that she didn't have to live with the past. She didn't have to relive it each and every day. Now she could move on. She knew it was Gott's will.

As they left the graveside, Emma gave the headstone a last glance and wondered what here future would hold?

Book Six: Amish Return

"Just so, I tell you, there will be more joy in heaven over one sinner who repents than over ninety-nine righteous persons who need no repentance." Luke 15:7

Jarron Williams and his father drove up to the store through the harsh blizzard outside. Emma Bontrager could see them out the window, spotting Jarron's familiar plaid jacket and auburn hair immediately.

"Emma, could you help me with this?" Sarah asked, sighing as she shifted Little Ruthie into her other arm.

The store was empty today, being a snowy Monday. Emma walked over to assist her elder sister, giving Ruthie a smile as the baby opened her big blue eyes. The little child had grown over the past few months, but she still was small in stature, with fine blonde hair sprouting from her head.

Sarah pointed to the cupboard below the moneybox. "There's some change in there—could you grab it?"

Emma bent down to retrieve the change, her stomach filling with butterflies. She hadn't felt like this since she had been courting her late husband, Eli Yoder, and the nervousness she now experienced made her frantic. She had never smiled so much as she had when she was with Jarron, ever since their reunion a couple of months ago.

He seemed determined to prove his sincerity. Although she had once felt some resentment toward him after he left without word to go to California with his wife, soon after promising Eli that he would take care of her and be her friend, he had come by every week or so to say hello to her. Sometimes they would go on long walks down the country road, when the weather was good. Other times Jarron would offer to relieve Sarah and help Emma with the store for a few hours.

But the feeling she felt now at the prospect of seeing Jarron again was more than just friendship. Instantly she scolded herself. Jarron was married, and certainly didn't see her in *that* way, as a special someone. She also felt a pang of guilt flow through her; she had loved Eli more than she had ever thought possible with any man. Betraying him by desiring someone else seemed wrong.

The bell of the door rang as Emma straightened quickly, forgetting to get the change and nearly bumping her head on the counter.

"Mr. Williams," Sarah greeted, her voice friendly. "And Jarron, how are you both today?"

"Just fine, Sarah," Jarron's father, Mr. Williams, replied. "Little Ruthie looks happy and healthy."

Sarah grinned, blushing a little at the mention of her baby. She loved talking about her children. The only vanity Emma knew her to have was to ramble on about her Isaac's talent in the barn, or Little Ruthie's attempts at sitting up. Emma didn't think that was so great a sin; family was the most important thing, after all.

As Sarah showed Mr. Williams the way to their new baked goods, Jarron leaned across the counter and gave her a smile. She clenched her hands, trying to get rid of some of her nerves.

"It's snowing like crazy out there," he said, nodding toward the window.

"*Ja*...I noticed this morning how deep the snow has gotten."

He leaned in a bit closer, lowering his voice. "It kind of reminds me of the first time we met. You remember?"

A smile played on her lips as flashes of memories flew through her mind. She, her younger sister Martha, and her beau Eli had walked through the snow toward Emile Smith's house to give him some Amish goodies. Eli had thrown a snowball at Martha, grinning as they teased each other. That day, Emma had met the *Englischer* Jarron.

She could still remember sitting in his truck with him, his lips hovering just inches from hers. That had been the moment that she had decided to join the Church. She knew she belonged with the Amish, the Plain folk. An *Englisch* life with Jarron would have been too fancy and ungodly for her.

His smile faded a little. "I forgot that Eli was there, too. I'm sorry for bringing up that memory."

She blinked, brought back to reality by his soothing voice. "Not only Eli, but Martha too," she said, smiling sadly at him. "It's *goed*, Jarron. I need to remember."

"You haven't heard from Martha?" he asked.

She shook her head. "Not since the last time she left."

Her sister had left to join the *Englisch* world at a young age, following her boyfriend into the unknown. They were engaged, as far as Emma knew. She tried not to think about it; she missed Martha dearly, but Martha never bothered with any of her family as she lived her life of fancy adventure. Emma thought that she could so easily have taken the path that Martha had chosen to tread. If their lips had touched in his truck that day, then she knew her path would have been a completely different journey. But, the lips didn't touch and now she was here, a young Amish widow and he was there, on the other side of the counter, an *Englischer* with his own wife. Although they were just on different sides of the counter, they could have been on different sides of the earth.

Jarron straightened a little as his father and Sarah wandered back to the counter. Mr. Williams had a few items in his hands. His wife liked homemade apple pies, and those were one of the store's specialties. Jarron rubbed his hand on the back of his neck.

"Emma," he said quietly. They moved out of the way of Sarah and Mr. Williams, who were chatting about children. "I have something I need to tell you."

Emma froze, her heart sinking a little. Was he going to leave her again, after all this time as friends? She wasn't sure if her heart could take any more loss. First Eli, then Martha—was Jarron the next to go?

"I want to tell you in private," he told her, glancing back over at his father as the man finished paying. "Tonight."

"Tonight?" she asked, but Mr. Williams was already walking toward the door.

"Jarron, you coming?" he asked his son, holding the door open. The cold winter breeze swept in and made Little Ruthie squirm in her mother's arms.

"Tonight," Jarron whispered, giving her a wink that made her blush all over again.

But he replied to the man who told him, "Who is my mother, and who are my brothers?" And stretching out his hand toward his disciples, he said, "Here are my mother and my brothers! For whoever does the will of my Father in heaven is my brother and sister and mother." Matthew 12:48-50

Darkness came earlier than usual, as Emma sat in the corner playing with Isaac. Sarah was in the chair, sewing up a pair of her husband, Jeremiah's, trousers. The man of the house himself was standing near the window, rocking Little Ruthie back and forth, trying to will her to sleep. He wasn't having much success.

Emma stifled a yawn. Ruthie was a crier at night, and since Emma had lived with her sister's family since Eli's death, she felt more than obligated to help with the child so her parents could have a good night's rest. Things had gotten worse lately, as Ruthie grew fussier and fussier. Emma wondered if the cold did that to babies. She didn't know. Now she would never get the opportunity to find out with her own children. Eli was gone, struck down by *Gott* so young. *Gott* had also decided not to bless them with a *boppli,* during their marriage. Now Eli would be gone forever, with no reminder of him running around playing with the other children. She started to think what kind of mother she would be? Would she have been as good as her own blessed mother? Again, she didn't know. And she never would.

Ruthie, grizzled a little more and Jeremiah glanced at Sarah with a look that suggested that they were in for a long night. Isaac, on the other hand, was a perfect angel. He had grown into a quiet young child, thoughtful and considerate to everyone and everything. His little hands fitted perfectly into Emma's as they played their game.

"*Ach*," Sarah said, standing, rubbing at her lower back. She had had back pain ever since Little Ruthie had been born, but refused to go see an *Englisch* physician. "I think it is time for me to go to bed. Come on, Isaac."

She scooped her son up, wincing a little as she balanced him on a hip, her other hand rubbing her back.

"Do you need any help?" Emma asked, looking up at her worriedly.

Sarah gave her a reassuring smile. "No, *zus*. I do love you for asking, but you've been more than enough of a help today."

Jeremiah followed her into their room that they shared with the babies. Emma sighed. Often she would stay up later than everyone else, sometimes enjoying her time alone, more often than not letting her mind float back to Eli. She missed him still, even now that Jarron was back in her life.

As she thought of Jarron she jumped up, grabbing a candle and chair and striding to the window. She peered out into the darkness, shivering a little at the sight of the frozen night. What had Jarron meant when he said he needed to tell her something tonight? Surely he wouldn't travel all the way out to Sarah and Jeremiah's house in this frigid blackness.

She sat down on the chair, placing the candle on the windowsill. She rocked back and forth, back and forth, lulling herself into sleep and embracing unconsciousness. In her dreams she could be with Eli again.

"A wife is bound to her husband as long as he lives. But if her husband dies, she is free to be married to whom she wishes, only in the Lord." Corinthians 7:39

She woke up shivering. Her candle had gone out. Her neck hurt from laying at an awkward angle, and the chair's hard back had dug into her flesh. She was still dressed, too, which only made her more uncomfortable.

Standing, Emma stretched out all the kinks in her muscles, ready to go to bed. Ruthie hadn't started crying yet, which made her hopeful for the rest of the evening—maybe the household would have an uninterrupted sleep tonight. Midnight wasn't far away. She should have gone to bed with the others. Falling asleep in a rocker always felt like a good idea, but it never turned out that way.

Emma jumped as something hit the window. Her heart began to race in fear. What was it? She squinted, seeing that a snowball had left its print on the glass.

"What..." she began in a whisper, as another snowball hit the window.

"Jarron," she breathed, crossing her arms across her chest and trying to gain some warmth. Butterflies filled her stomach again, and she shoved them down, willing them to be still.

It was midnight and Jarron had actually come. In the middle of the blizzard he had come. What did he want? Why did he have to met her at this hour? A thousand questions filled her confused mind. Another snowball hit the window lightly as if to remind her. She flew toward the door, pulling on her coat, boots, and bonnet. Taking a deep breath, she strode out into the cold.

She couldn't make out Jarron, but his red truck was impossible to miss even in the blackness. She made her way as quickly as possible towards it.

The heated cab felt like a breath of summer air as Emma climbed into the big red truck, tugging the door shut behind her. She heard him laugh, the deep, guttural sound filling her and making her heart pump a little faster.

"You look like a snow monster!" he teased, brushing some of the snowflakes that had settled on her shoulders away.

She giggled, surprised that the sound came from her. When was the last time she had felt this happy? She couldn't remember. But the pleasant sensation was mixed yet again with the sense of guilt. Always, she felt as if she should still grieve Eli. She tried to ignore the feeling, consciously realizing that her smile had faded a little.

He didn't seem to notice. "I want to take you somewhere. Don't get angry, okay?"

"Angry?" She looked at him, puzzled, but he had already pulled on his winter hat and put the truck into gear.

They went slowly down the icy road. Emma looked out the window, smiling up at the moon. In the past, she would have never dreamed that she'd be out in the middle of the night with an *Englischer*. But Eli's death had changed things. It had changed her. As much as she felt the need to remain loyal to Eli forever, she knew that he had always admired her spirit. A wonderful-good woman, he used to call her. He wouldn't have wanted her to give that up.

She had been grieving him so long she felt as if she hadn't experienced happiness, true happiness, in years. Being with Jarron made her feel more alive. And she had to admit something deeper was shared between them, too, though she couldn't quite figure that part out yet. Long ago, she had dug a deep pit in her heart where God had used to reside. After Eli's death, that pit had grown larger, threatening to swallow her up in bitterness. Jarron had begun to fill that hole, with his positivity and constant presence in her life.

"What does your wife think of you driving out and about at this late hour?" she tried starting a conversation.

He gave her a sad look. "I need to talk to you about that. And about other things."

"*Ja*?" A sliver of worry crept into her mind, wondering what he wanted to tell her that could have warranted this late-night excursion.

"Soon," was all he said, continuing to drive along in silence.

She recognized where they were before they even pulled up to the old house. Tucked away behind the house, the new-looking barn stood, its frame darker than the dim blue sky. Eli's barn. "*Niet*," she said, shaking her head. Her hands trembled as she looked down at them, not wanting to face her past like this. "No, Jarron."

He stopped the truck and switched off the headlights, but Emma could still see the outline of her and Eli's first and only home together. She could feel tears sting her eyes.

"Why did you bring me here?" she asked, her voice hoarse with emotion.

He grabbed her hand, not letting her pull away, to sink inside herself, into that dark place that she reserved for grieving Eli's loss. "Emma, I know how much you still miss him. It's okay to grieve."

A few tears escaped her eyes. She never wanted to forget Eli, but she didn't want to be controlled by her grief as she had in the past, either. Jarron sighed and pulled off a glove, his warm fingers brushing up against her cheek and wiping away some of her tears.

"I have to tell you something," he told her. "I can only do it here. Will you come with me?"

"I will tell of your name to my brothers; in the midst of the congregation I will praise you." Psalm 22:22

It didn't take much thinking about. Of course she was coming with him. She nodded, trusting him implicitly. He looked at her seriously, pulling back on his glove and climbing out of the truck. She followed suit, glad when he took her hand, lending her some of his strength.

They trudged through the deep snow. She nearly fell over from the cold wind, swaying a little as she tried to regain her balance. They neared the barn, where the goats and farm animals had once resided. They had only a small lot of them, but it had been a start. In time they had planned for bigger and better things. At least Eli did. The thought of him, hurt like a knife in the stomach. This was Eli's barn. She didn't feel right being here with Jarron, on this cold, starless night.

As they drew close to the building, the wind settled, blocked by the sturdy Englisch-manufactured wood. Jarron stopped suddenly, turning toward her. His fingers were still wrapped tightly around hers. Clouds puffed out of his mouth as he breathed through his mouth, his voice so quiet she could hardly hear it.

"Emma, you have to promise me that you won't say a word when we go inside."

"What? What's going on?" she asked, frowning at his secrecy.

"Just..." he hesitated. "Just trust me, okay?"

She bit her lip, fear filling her at what they might find beyond the door of the barn. "*Ja.*"

He opened the door a crack. She realized the barn was lit by the soft glow of a candle or two. He stepped aside so she could peer in.

With a gasp, she jumped backward, nearly falling into the snow. Jarron pressed a finger up against her lips, and she stared at him with wide eyes.

"Not a word, remember?"

She brushed past him again, peeking into the little slit of light. In the middle of Eli's barn, near where they had used to keep the goats, a small bundle was curled up in a few ragged blankets. The light in the room flickered a little. She realized the glow came from a single, nearly dead, candle.

The only part of the bundle that told her it was human was the short, chopped off, pure black hair.

"Who's that? What are they doing here in Eli's barn," Emma spat at Jarron. But he just smiled back at her. The bundle turned over, and suddenly they was a flash of realization in Emma's mind.

"It's Martha," she breathed, bringing her hands to her mouth. Had Martha really been living in Eli's barn? Had Eli somehow sent Martha to her?

Jarron's fingers wrapped gently around her arm, pulling her back so he could close the door. "I found her the other day, when I came to check up on the place. She tried to make me promise not to tell you."

"But why?" she asked, astonished. "If she couldn't come to me, why not Mam or Dat or Sarah? Why is she hiding in here? How long has this gone on?"

"I don't know," he admitted. "She wouldn't tell me anything. All I know is that she's sick, Em."

"Sick?"

He nodded. "She's really thin. I don't think she's been eating enough."

Tears filled Emma's eyes, hot against her cold face. "What should we do?"

"That's up to you. I'm willing to help you. She needs help—maybe a doctor—"

"No," Emma pleaded with him. She shivered as she thought about Eli, in the sterile Englisch hospital, dying alone. "No, I don't want her near a doctor."

Any anger she had pent up toward Martha had dissipated. She felt as if a great weight had been lifted off her chest. Although she knew that it would likely resurface once the novelty of Martha returning had worn off, she enjoyed the feeling of pure love, pure forgiveness. Perhaps Jarron was meant to heal her heart in more than one way.

She looked up toward the sky, wondering if *Gott* Himself had put Jarron back in her life for a reason. If Martha had shown up at Eli's barn because of *Gott's* Will. She didn't know. The empty space in her heart began to fill, a little, but she didn't let herself get carried away. *Lord, if it is You who have done this deed, I thank you*, she prayed. She hadn't prayed in months, not really. Not since Eli's sickness became clear.

He frowned, rubbing his forehead in thought. "I don't know, then. Maybe we should just wait—she'll come to you if she needs help, right?"

Emma thought for a moment, then shook her head. "I can't leave her in this barn another night. She is my sister, Amish or *Englisch.* Thank you, Jarron, for showing me to her."

She moved past him, reaching for the barn door. He caught her arm again. She could see the dim light from the sky reflecting off his eyes. "Em, I have one more thing to tell you. I know right now isn't the best time, but..."

"Jarron, I already know," she said, intending to give him a quick hug, to thank him for bringing her to her sister. As she went to pull away, he wrapped his arms tightly around her, the warmth of his body pressing up against hers.

"You do?"

She nodded as warmth filled her body, reawakening her senses as they had been before Eli's death. She could smell the scents of sap and dirt on his coat. She pulled away, face flushed. "I know you're married, and even if you weren't..." she hesitated a little, not wanting to say her next words but knowing that they had to be said. It wasn't fair of her to tempt him from his wife, to promise him something she could not give. "Even if you weren't married, we could never be together, anyway. I like being friends, Jarron."

His face fell a little, but he nodded all the same. "Well, that's that, then." His voice revealed nothing, no trace of emotion.

Her heart sank a little at his reaction. Had she just said something majorly wrong?

She opened her mouth to say something when a small, shrill voice raced through the air. "Who's there?"

Jarron nodded at her as she opened the door. Martha was awake now, standing up against the corner of the barn, the melted candle in her hand. She shivered, her entire body shaking as she peered into the darkness, trying to get the fading candle's light to illuminate the other side of the room.

Despite the dimness of the light, Emma could see the deep, shallow shadows and lines of her sister's face. She had wrapped herself up in one of the tattered blankets, but Emma could see how extremely thin she was. She dressed in *Englisch* clothes, in a sweatshirt and jeans. Her hair was her natural color once more, but it was cut and shorn in different places.

"Martha, it's Emma." Emma could feel Jarron at her back, his hand touching her shoulder gently in support. Tears drifted down her face. "It's your sister."

Martha ran to her.

Book Seven: Amish Family

"Jesus then said to them, "Truly, truly, I say to you, it was not Moses who gave you the bread from heaven, but my Father gives you the true bread from heaven. For the bread of God is he who comes down from heaven and gives life to the world." They said to him, "Sir, give us this bread always." Jesus said to them, "I am the bread of life; whoever comes to me shall not hunger, and whoever believes in me shall never thirst." John 6:50-71

"I'm not hungry." Martha pushed the basket of food away, leaning her head tiredly down on the table.

Emma sat down with a weary sigh of her own. Nearly two weeks had passed since her sister's unannounced return, and things hadn't improved. Although Emma had convinced her to stay in her old home, Martha remained stubbornly too thin and lonely for her liking.

She looked around the tiny kitchen, her mind filling with memories. In a way, having Martha stay in the house she had once shared with her husband, Eli, was good for her—it made Emma face her past. After Eli's death, she had almost been afraid to return to the house, scared that her memories would be too overwhelming.

Yes, she remembered things, but not all her memories were of Eli's gaunt face and frail body, how he had looked as he neared the end. Instead she thought of cooking dinner as he sat at this very same kitchen table, smelling of dirt and work. He'd sometimes get up and help her, wrapping his arms around her waist and giving her a sweet kiss on the cheek.

She still couldn't bring herself to enter their room, a place where Eli had been often when he was sick. But she could now walk into the house without feeling that niggling, horrid feeling of fear, and for that she was glad.

"There's some baked *kip* in there," Emma tried, watching her sister. "And some *brood* Sarah baked the other day."

Martha popped her head up. "Does she know you took it?"

Emma shook her head honestly. "Sarah doesn't know you're back, Martha. No one does, except Jarron and me."

Martha relaxed. Emma frowned, not understanding why she didn't want anyone, not even Mamm and Daed, to know she was back. It had been years since any of them had seen her, and the time apart had clearly not been good for her. Today she wore a few layers and jeans, topped off with a blue Englisch sweatshirt that said "Anchorage" on the front of it. Even through the layers Emma could see her sister's bony frame. She needed to eat.

"Martha, you have to eat."

"Emma, stop." Her tone was hurt, verging on crying.

Martha got up from the table, heading toward Emma's old room to go and lie down. Where once Martha had been full of life, so happy to be a part of the Englisch world, the life seemed to have been drained out of her, leaving behind a shell of what she once was. Emma could remember a time when she used to take pride in her jet black hair, all brushed out and reaching toward the ground, but her hair had been cut and now stood at awkward angles, short and unkempt.

Emma sighed, standing to go and check on her other baskets she had brought this week. One loaf of bread had a few bites taken out of it, but all the rest of the food was untouched.

She took a few steps toward her old bedroom, determined to find out what was wrong with Martha. A cold fear overtook her. She couldn't go back in that room, yet. There were too many haunting memories, and she didn't feel her faith in Gott wasn't quite that strong.

"Fear not, for I am with you; be not dismayed, for I am your God; I will strengthen you, I will help you, I will uphold you with my righteous right hand." - Isaiah 41:10

Jarron Williams, the Englischer, came to the service on Sunday. Emma sat with her sister Sarah and her family as usual, but she felt someone brush up against her shoulder and looked over to find Jarron Williams.

"*Hallo*, Jarron," Sarah said, smiling happily. She had her daughter, Little Ruthie, in her arms. The baby gurgled a greeting.

"Sarah," Jarron nodded to her in greeting, then to her husband, Jeremiah, who had hold of their son Isaac. "Jeremiah, you are well?"

"*Ja*, just waiting for this cold to go away," Jeremiah replied, laughing. Isaac, who often imitated his father, laughed along too. Emma hid a smile.

"Me too," Jarron admitted, giving him a grin. As soon as he had said his greeting to her relatives, he lowered her voice. "Hi, Em."

Emma lowered her eyes, blushing a little at his use of her nickname. Not many Englishers ever wanted to go to the Amish service, but Jarron and Preacher Amos had a good relationship, and Amos appreciated Jarron's fascination with their culture. Emma didn't mind, of course, though she could feel the stares as she stood next to the Englischer, chatting with him before Amos began speaking.

Do they think we are having an affair? she thought, worried. Jarron was married; she wouldn't dream of trying to break up his marriage for her own gain, even if she was fond of Jarron. She wasn't sure why Jarron kept attending their service, but she was happy to have him there.

"How's Martha doing?" he asked, his voice almost in a whisper.

"*Ach*, not well," she responded in an equally low voice.

Jarron glanced at her. "Still not eating?"

She shook her head. "Not a bite."

"Maybe I could help?"

Emma thought for a moment, then shrugged. "She does respect you. Maybe if you came out..." she stopped herself, feeling guilt slice through her. She knew that she wasn't trying to get Jarron to come out because of Martha. Ever since their night at the barn, Emma had felt closer to him. She trusted him.

But he was still married. She had to struggle to remember that.

"I can come out," Jarron said. "How about right after church? We can go together."

His words sent a slight chill down her spine. She didn't have time to answer, as Amos stood above the tiny congregation, beginning to speak to begin the service.

"So put away all malice and all deceit and hypocrisy and envy and all slander. Like newborn infants, long for the pure spiritual milk, that by it you may grow up into salvation— if indeed you have tasted that the Lord is good. As you come to him, a living stone rejected by men but in the sight of God chosen and precious, you yourselves like living stones are being built up as a spiritual house, to be a holy priesthood, to offer spiritual sacrifices acceptable to God through Jesus Christ. ..." Peter 2:1-12

"I'll catch up," Emma told Jarron as they walked out of the house after the service. He nodded, saying his goodbyes to Isaac, who had only just begun to talk and kept saying "Bye bye."

Sarah's vice-like grip on her arm tugged her away. "Emma, Jarron is married."

Emma gave her a frown, tugging her arm out of her grasp. "I know that, Sarah."

"Well, I've noticed you've been gone a lot lately. It is against our ways to court an Englischer, even if Jarron wasn't married." Sarah gave her a disapproving look. "I know you miss Eli, Emma...but running off with Jarron Williams..."

"Stop," Emma snapped, softening her tone when she realized how angry she sounded. Sarah had no idea where Emma had been going off to, and it certainly hadn't been to see Jarron, but Emma couldn't blame her sister being concerned. She might have thought the same thing, if she hadn't known about Martha. "Sarah, I promise you, I haven't been going off to see Jarron."

"Then where *have* you been going?" Sarah asked, still suspicious.

Emma wanted to respect Martha's wishes and not tell others about her return, but at the same time, she didn't feel right lying to Sarah. Of all people, Sarah had been there when she needed her most, after Eli's death. She had been living with Sarah for years now, a part of her family, and Sarah had never once complained.

She struggled to find words. "I've been going out to Eli's old barn, tidying up." It wasn't exactly a lie, but it wasn't entirely true, either. "I know he would have wanted it that way."

Sarah looked a little deflated, cradling the sleeping Ruthie a little bit more firmly. "*Ach*, I'm sorry, Emma. I just don't want you to get in trouble."

I'm not the one in trouble, Emma thought, but just smiled and nodded. She appreciated her sister's concern, but still couldn't tell her the full truth, not yet. She wanted Martha to trust her again, to confide in her so she could help her sister become well again. Telling Sarah would only ruin the trust she had managed to glean.

"Jarron is going to take me out to the barn," she explained to Sarah. "The snow's too deep today and his truck is heated."

Sarah gave her a skeptical look. "I don't know about that, Emma, but if you think that's what you need to do, I cannot hold you back."

Emma grinned, giving her sister a kiss on the cheek. Although Sarah hadn't expressed her approval, she wasn't going to try and stop Emma from going with Jarron, and for that she was grateful. "*Danki*, Sarah."

She could see Sarah's lips twisting up into a light grin, though she tried to look stern.

"There is no fear in love, but perfect love casts out fear. For fear has to do with punishment, and whoever fears has not been perfected in love." - John 4:18

Martha was gone when they arrived.

"Where could she have gone?" Jarron asked, watching as Emma looked through the house frantically, even taking a chance and peeping into her old room.

She stopped looking, turning toward him. "I don't know."

Jarron rubbed the back of his neck, thinking. "Maybe she went to your Mamm and Daed's?"

"I don't know," she said in despair, sitting down heavily in the kitchen chair. "Why wouldn't she at least tell me, first? You don't think she ran away again, do you?"

Jarron thought for a moment, sitting down next to her. "I don't think so. She seemed pretty fed up with Englisch life."

"We can't go over to my Mamm and Daed's house, especially if it turns out she isn't there. They'll think something is wrong, or that we..." Emma lowered her eyes, biting her lip against saying what she wanted to.

"That we're having an affair?"

"*Ja,*" she admitted. "It isn't right for a Plain girl to be with an Englisch man by herself, anyway, and the fact that you're married..."

Jarron looked at her, then looked down at the table, his eyes traveling back up to her in disbelief. "What?"

"You're married," Emma repeated, confused at his strange reaction.

"I'm not married, Emma. I thought you knew—I was going to tell you at the barn that night that I showed you where Martha was, and then you acted like you had already heard about the divorce, and you said it wouldn't matter anyway."

Emma consciously closed her gaping mouth. She hadn't known Jarron was divorced, and now everything had changed. She wasn't sure how to respond at all. Jarron stared at her, waiting for her reaction, but she couldn't think of anything to say or do. He reached over, taking her hand in his, his eyes finding hers.

The door flew open, and Martha walked in, shivering from the cold.

"*Ach!* Where have you been?" Emma snatched her hand away from Jarron's, shaking a little. She didn't know if her trembles were from her sister returning so suddenly or from holding Jarron's hand—she didn't want to think about it.

"I went for a walk," Martha said, looking from Emma to Jarron, then back to Emma. "Am I interrupting something?"

Emma could feel her face flush at her sister's observation.

"Not at all," Jarron offered. "We were just looking for you, Martha."

"Well, you found me."

Martha didn't smile. Emma didn't think she had smiled, really smiled, in a long time. "Did you go to Mamm and Daed's?" she asked.

"Emma, I'm not going to their house. Stop asking me that, please!" Tears sparkled in Martha's eyes as she brushed past them both and went into the bedroom.

Emma stood, intending on following her. She felt a warm hand on her shoulder. Jarron shook his head. "Let her be. She's dealing with things in her own way."

"But it is not the right way," Emma protested. "She needs to talk with us, so we can help her."

Jarron gave her a sad smile. "Sometimes you have to let people figure out things in their own time, Em."

Emma looked at him, curious if he was talking about something that had happened in his own life, with his ex-wife. He revealed nothing more to her.

"I think I'll stay here tonight," Emma told him. "Would you mind giving me a lift back to Sarah's so I can get some things?"

"For the Lord will not forsake his people; he will not abandon his heritage;" - Psalm 94:14

They were silent as they bumped along the road. Emma kept her hands tightly clenched in her lap, willing herself not to look at Jarron.

Suddenly, Jarron laughed. "Is this awkward?"

Emma didn't answer, not wanting to be rude. Jarron got the hint, though, and laughed again. The sound made Emma smile a little—she had always enjoyed Jarron's laugh.

"This is silly, Em. We've been friends for years. We've gone through tons of trials together. Why does our relationship have to be awkward now?"

Because, Emma wanted to say, *what I feel for you is more than friendship, Jarron*. And she did. At first she had felt guilty, wanting to stay true to Eli even after he had died. But Jarron and her friendship had blossomed and grown, blooming into something a little more, perhaps something that Eli might have even approved of, watching over her as he did now.

Still, Emma could feel a pit growing in her stomach, almost wishing that Jarron hadn't told her that he had ended it with his Englisch wife. How could Emma's relationship with him progress, anyway? She couldn't even court any Englischer, let alone a divorcee.

The snow outside landed on Jarron's windshield, the big, fat flakes sticking to the glass. Jarron flipped on the windshield wipers. Evening was coming soon. No doubt Sarah would be full of questions when she got home, but Emma intended on simply grabbing her things and making her way back to her old house, where Martha was. She didn't trust Martha to be alone right now—and truth be told, she didn't know how to handle her sister's situation any more than she did Jarron.

"Thank you for the ride, Jarron," she said.

He grabbed her arm gently before she could climb out of the cab. "You need anything else, Em? Are you sure you can make it through the snow?"

She shrugged. "I got some new boots this year. It shouldn't be a problem."

He looked like he wanted to say something more, his grip tightening a little on her arm before letting go. "Emma, I..."

"*Ja?*" she asked, twisting her hands nervously as she leaned a little closer to him. She could smell a slight hint of some type of artificial Englisch scent on him, a manly scent.

"I just want you to know, I'm here for you. And if you ever change your mind—about courting an Englisch man, that is—well, I'll still be here."

Emma could feel her face turning dozens of shades of red. He let go of her arm, and she climbed out of the cab, welcoming the cold breeze on her flushed cheeks.

She did the only thing she knew how to do, her go-to action for most everything, especially in her younger years.

She said some polite goodbyes and ran.

**"And you will know the truth, and the truth will set you free."
John 8:32**

Emma shook a little as she began to pack a few clothes, sneaking in some food. Sarah stood at the doorway, Isaac following his mother like usual.

"Where are you going, Emma?"

Emma looked up from her clothes, tears filling her eyes. The frustration of the day and the emotion she hadn't felt before when Martha had disappeared had filled her, especially now that Jarron, who was her constant comfort, had gone. She almost wished she had asked him to wait, to stay the night with her and Martha, just so she'd have some backup in case Martha decided to open up to her.

How could she deal with Martha's illness by herself? She had tried to save Eli, tried as hard as she could, but she hadn't been able to save him. Would she even be able to save her sister?

"Emma, you look troubled." Sarah frowned, taking her sister by the hand and sitting down on the edge of the bed. "What's wrong?"

"I don't know if I should tell you." The words popped out of her mouth through their own accord, as if someone—or something—spurred her forward.

"Of course you should tell me, dear. We must be honest with each other, *ja*?"

Tears spilled from Emma's eyes as her lips formed the words that had to be said. She told Sarah everything about Martha, how she had come back only a shell of who she once was, how her joy and youthfulness had disappeared, how she was too thin and still refused to eat.

"She has so many secrets, Sarah. I don't even know where to begin. I'm so frightened."

Sarah enveloped her in a hug. Isaac toddled into the room, putting his little hand on Emma's lap.

"Why are you crying, Auntie?"

Emma looked down through glassy eyes and scooped Isaac up in a hug, taking comfort in his familiar baby smell. She hugged him until he began to squirm, then she put him down with a laugh.

"I need to see her," Sarah said, watching her son as he played and talked to himself.

"She told me not to tell anyone. I don't know if you being there would make her run away."

Sarah shook her head. "It doesn't matter, Emma. We're all Bontragers. We must stick together."

She stood. Emma had never seen her look more determined, or fierce. She looked down at Emma seriously. "I'm going to pack up a few things. Jeremiah can watch the children. We'll take the buggy."

Before she could say a word, her sister strode out of the room. Emma bit her lip, wondering if she had done the right thing by telling Sarah about Martha's return. Perhaps this was Gott's way of giving her an answer to her problem, a way to help Martha.

"She is more precious than jewels, and nothing you desire can compare with her." Proverbs 3:15

Sarah had a way with people that Emma had never possessed. She walked straight into Emma's old bedroom, and soon Emma could hear Martha's surprised voice. The girl never came out of the room, though, and Emma didn't want to interfere.

Instead she set herself about dusting up the kitchen and small living area, lighting the candles they had brought so they had a warm, soft glow about the room. She paused a few times as she heard a few sobs coming from inside the room, but Sarah hadn't called her in yet, so she stayed where she was.

She stopped by the window, looking out into the dark cold night. On many occasions, she could remembering standing at this same window, watching as the crews, Amish and Englisch, helped to put up Eli's barn when he was too ill to do so. Tonight she couldn't even see the outline of the big building, the moon hidden by the clouds as the snow continued to fall down.

Ach, Eli, I do miss you. She missed him more than anyone or anything in this earth, but she knew he would want her to move on, to be happy with her life. Jarron's offer still stood in her mind, weighing her heart down with a decision that needed to be made. But how could a relationship with him ever work? He was Englisch, she was Plain. She was committed to the Church, even if her faith had been sorely tested. She belonged with her family, with her sisters.

But why, then, was her heart fighting against what she knew to be right?

A flash of light caught her eye, and she peered through the window, squinting a little to see what was happening. A small pocket of glowing light emerged in the darkness, behind the window of the barn.

Emma's heart beat in her ears loudly—who was in Eli's barn this late at night? She strode toward the closed door of her room, intending to alert Sarah about the intruder, but she could hear Martha's voice talking more than she had heard in a long while.

Setting her jaw and grabbing a frying pan from the cupboard, just in case she had to defend herself, she braved the cold, heading toward the light in the darkness.

To be continued....

Book Eight: Amish Unity

"Love is patient and kind; love does not envy or boast; it is not arrogant or rude. It does not insist on its own way; it is not irritable or resentful; it does not rejoice at wrongdoing, but rejoices with the truth. Love bears all things, believes all things, hopes all things, endures all things." Corinthians 13:4-7

Jarron turned around to look at her, startled as she walked in. Emma gaped at him, shocked that he was in Eli's barn at such a late hour. From the glow of the small flashlight he had set up facing the ceiling, she could see the shiny liquid of tears on his cheeks. He turned away, embarrassed, wiping his face with the back of his sleeves.

"Sorry, Emma, did I surprise you?"

Emma stole into the barn the rest of the way, closing the door against the cold winter wind behind her. "Jarron, what are you doing here? It's so late, and..."

He sniffled a little, turning back toward her now that he had cleaned his face up. She could see the slight stubble on his chin, his eyes taking her face in. "I don't know... I was worried about things, the last time we parted." He hesitated, his eyes lowering to the ground. "I thought maybe Eli could provide me with answers."

She nodded. She could understand Jarron's desire to be in this place, the place where her late husband Eli had spent so much of his time and hopes on. Often she herself could almost feel Eli's comforting presence in this place. She looked up at the sturdy barn's rafters, noticing the cobwebs that lined the beams. Eli wouldn't have liked that. She really should have come by to clean, after he had died. But Emma couldn't stand to be in her old home alone, now that Eli was gone, much less the barn, which had once been filled with the sounds and smells of animals and hay, only to be reduced to an empty building now.

Jarron sighed, rubbing his eyes tiredly. "I miss him."

Emma could feel a lump growing in her throat, even after these past years of living without Eli. "*Ja,* me too."

"I promised him I would take care of you, and then I ran away..." She had never heard Jarron's voice shake in the way it did now, with pure emotion. His eyes locked on hers, trying to unsuccessfully fight back his tears. "And now I don't know if anything can be the same between us, Emma."

She stared at him, confused, talking a few steps further as if her presence would help calm him down. Jarron had never been one to show much emotion around her, but he was a man broken, now. "Whatever do you mean? Nothing has changed, Jarron..."

"It has," he insisted. "I don't think you understand. I love you, Emma Bontrager. Even when you were married to Eli...I loved you, sinner as I am. It was part of the reason I ran away, even part of the reason I got married to someone else."

Emma reached out, grabbing a support beam to steady herself. Jarron had hinted that he'd court her if it was permissible, but what he was saying now were words she had never heard from any man, much less an Englischer like Jarron.

He couldn't stop himself, it seemed. He took a few steps closer, tears streaming down his face. "I never would have taken you from Eli. I loved him like a brother, and he was one of my best friends. But even that couldn't stop me from loving you, Emma. I thought my time away would make my feelings for you disappear, but every time I'm around you they just get stronger and stronger."

Oh, Lord, please tell me the right thing to say? Emma found herself tongue-tied, praying for an answer. In her community, courting an Englischer was out of the question, but having Jarron confirm the exact same feelings she had been feeling lately made her want to tell him how she felt, too. But she held herself back, not willing to crush him by saying that she loved him, too. How would they ever be together, after all?

He sunk to his knees, still crying. She could feel his arms wrap around her waist as he buried his face in her skirts. "I don't know what the right thing to do is, Em, I don't. All I know is I can't live without you anymore. I want you to be mine, forever."

"Jarron, what are you saying?" She didn't try to escape from his grasp, feeling heat and tingles rush all along her body at his touch, at his warmth.

"I want to marry you, Em. I don't know if this is the way Eli would have wanted it, but I can't hold back my feelings any longer. I need you..." He looked up, as if pleading with her. "Please, Em."

She could feel her vision blur at his words, at what he was implying. She had known Jarron for so long, and they had been through so much together. She didn't have trouble seeing them together in the future, but was it a sin to love an Englischer? She had just barely reestablished her relationship with Gott—what if He didn't approve? How could she be sure that this was His will?

Instead of answering him, she knelt down, wrapping her arms around him. He hugged her back, tightly. The wind whistled through the small cracks of the barn, reminding Emma of how the winter lurked outside, spreading its frigid coldness in contrast to the warmth of Jarron, which encompassed her.

He drew away, wiping his nose with the back of his sleeve and laughing at himself. "I don't think I've ever cried this much in my life."

She gave him a grin. The warmth that had been building in her chest radiated outward, filling her with an emotion that she hadn't experienced for years. As she looked at Jarron, she could see her future, a way out of her troubled past. He had given her a choice once, so long ago, and she had chosen to stay with the Plain folk, marrying Eli instead. But now that Eli was gone, what was stopping her from moving on?

"Jarron, I..."

He looked at her, reaching over to touch her cheek with his cool fingers. She forgot to breathe as his thumb caressed her face, his eyes taking her in once more.

"I think I love you, too."

He smiled at her, hardly able to speak for a moment. Emma could feel joy bubbling up inside of her, a joy that she hadn't felt in such a long time. She loved Jarron Williams, and that was that. She had spent years grieving Eli, and knew he would have wanted her to be happy.

Jarron stood, taking her by the hand and helping her up before enveloping her in a hug once more. "Emma, do you want to make this work? I mean, really work?"

She nodded, burying her face in the fabric of his shirt, feeling safe in his arms. She didn't want to be alone, not anymore.

"Then we've got to find a way. I'm not going to lose you again."

"I appeal to you, brothers, by the name of our Lord Jesus Christ, that all of you agree, and that there be no divisions among you, but that you be united in the same mind and the same judgment."
Corinthians 1:10

Emma woke to the smell of breakfast in the kitchen. She stretched, working the kinks out of her back from sleeping on the floor all night, curled up in a few blankets as was usual when she stayed at her own home.

Her elder sister, Sarah, stood at the stove, baking away as the morning hours crept forward. She heard Emma stir and turned toward her, giving her a grin.

Emma sat up, the memories of the night before fresh in her mind. She had been so filled with excitement and joy that once Jarron had left with the promise he would return to speak with her, she had hardly been able to sleep at all. Now, with the morning settling in, she'd had a chance to think about what was to be done about the situation between her and Jarron. It was against the Amish ways to court an Englischer once pledged to the Church, and she wasn't Martha—she wasn't ready or willing to run off with Jarron, though the thought had crossed her mind once or twice. But her family was important to her, too, perhaps more important than her own happiness.

Jarron had said he needed her, but her family needed her, too. She could never dream of leaving them, but she didn't want to lose Jarron, either.

"Good morning," Sarah said, turning back toward the oven. "You'd best get ready for the service."

Emma gasped. She had forgotten it was Sunday. Sarah was likely preparing breakfast so she wouldn't have to do it later, after church. Getting up, she winced a little. The floor wasn't exactly the most comfortable place to sleep.

"Could you wake Martha?" Sarah asked.

"What for?" Emma gave her a confused look.

Since their younger sister, Martha, had returned from the Englisch world, Emma had been battling with Martha's thinness and unwillingness to reengage with the community. Martha hadn't been baptized when she had left the community, but her homecoming would cause waves, for sure, especially with Mamm and Daed, who still didn't know that Martha had returned. Last Emma had known, Martha didn't seem particularly enthused to tell anyone about her reappearance. But ever since Emma had told Sarah about Martha's return, Martha had seemed to open up a little more.

"She has agreed to come to the service with us." Sarah looked at her as if to tell her not to inquire any further.

Emma took the hint and walked to her and Eli's old room, where Martha had been sleeping since she had shown up in Eli's barn weeks earlier. When she opened the door, she was surprised to see Martha dressed, brushing her chopped-up hair out. Today she wore a blouse and Englisch jeans, rather than her usual baggy sweatshirt and pants.

"Sarah says to get ready for the service."

Martha looked up, jumping, as if she had been interrupted from a deep thought. "I'm almost ready."

Emma gave her a small grin, relief flooding through her. For once, Martha's eyes didn't look so dead. She could see nervousness written on her sister's face, but she didn't want to pry into Martha's business.

Instead, Martha stopped her from leaving.

"Emma..." She hesitated, running the brush through her hair again. "Mamm and Daed will be there, won't they?"

"*Ja*," Emma said, nodding. "But so will Sarah and I. We're your sisters, Martha. We will support you no matter what."

"And Jarron? Will he be there?"

Emma thought for a moment. Jarron had been attending services on and off lately, being on good terms with Bishop Amos. "*Ja*, I believe so. He had been coming lately."

"Good. I don't want to look like the only Englischer there."

Emma nodded, heading toward the door. She didn't want to push Martha or step on her toes, but as she reached the doorframe, she turned around again, biting her lip.

"Martha, would you like a dress to wear? I mean..."

Martha shook her head, and Emma cringed, expecting an outburst, but her sister remained surprisingly calm. "No, thank you, Emma. I don't think I'm ready to go back to that just yet. I need to speak with the Bishop, first. And with Mamm and Daed. And, Emma?" Martha's blue eyes found hers. She still looked so pale and gaunt, but for the first time since her return Emma could see a bit of fierceness, a will to live, in her eyes. Whatever Sarah had said to her the night before must have worked. "Thank you, for everything. I wouldn't be here if it wasn't for you."

"What are sisters for?" Emma asked, giving her a wink.

Martha bit her lip. "I haven't been a good sister to you. How could you even forgive me for leaving like I did after Eli's death?"

Emma sighed, leaning up against the door and looking over at Martha. "It took me a long time to forgive you. But I don't think Gott wants us to hold grudges, Martha."

Her sister sighed, playing with the brush in her hands idly. "Sometimes I don't think Gott is real, Emma."

Emma frowned a little, coming over and sitting by Martha on the bed. "I was at that same place when Eli died. But I think it is normal for people to start doubting Gott and his will for us when times get hard. We just have to find ways to overcome our anger and doubt and trust in Him again."

"I've lost people too. I lost Eric, the man who I was supposed to marry—" Martha's voice cracked a little, wavering as she continued. "And he ran away with someone else. And I lost everyone else, too, when I ran away from here. I wish I'd done things differently, truly."

"It isn't too late to come back." Emma took her sister's hand in her own, watching as the girl tried to stifle back her tears. "You are still a Bontrager, Martha, and Gott has not forsaken you. You'll see."

Martha gave her a teary smile, suddenly grabbing her in a hug. "I hope you're right, Emma. I want to begin to heal, like you."

They heard a noise at the doorway, and turned to find Sarah beaming at them.

"My beautiful sisters," Sarah said happily, clapping her hands together excitedly. "Let's get going—we're going to be late."

"Praise the Lord! Praise God in his sanctuary; praise him in his mighty heavens! Praise him for his mighty deeds; praise him according to his excellent greatness! Praise him with trumpet sound; praise him with lute and harp! Praise him with tambourine and dance; praise him with strings and pipe! Praise him with sounding cymbals; praise him with loud clashing cymbals! ..." Psalm 150: 1-6

Most people had made it through the snow and ice to the service today, their wet clothing and warm bodies mingling together in a sort of comforting presence.

Emma looked around, trying to find Jarron, but she couldn't see him at all. Next to her stood Martha, sandwiched between Sarah and herself, trying to make herself look as small as possible. Sarah waved over Mamm and Daed when they arrived, as well as her own husband and children.

From the beginning, Emma could hear the whispers about her sister, but everyone seemed to put on a friendly face toward Martha, despite her Englisch attire. She hadn't been shunned, after all, so it was appropriate to treat her with every courtesy.

When Mamm and Daed arrived, everyone could hear the sharp sob that Mamm elicited upon seeing her youngest daughter. She practically ran over to Martha, embracing her instantly, as if she didn't notice how thin the girl had gotten. Emma could see Daed trailing behind, a look of bewilderment on his face. She had no doubt that Daed was happy to have Martha back, too. Finally their family was whole again, and the feeling felt wonderful after all these years of separation.

Bishop Amos emerged from a back room, and everyone quieted down to hear what he had to say. Emma could hardly pay attention to the preacher's words. Where was Jarron? Had he already changed his mind about her? Fear sliced through her mind—what if he had left again? Had everything he said been a lie?

Chewing on her lower lip, Emma tried to stay focused, not wanting to give into the spirit of fear that had filled her. She couldn't help but to think that Jarron had finally thought about what had happened last night, the impossibility of the situation making him not want to be with her any longer. She couldn't believe she had been so foolish as to think that they would be able to spend their lives together, especially when they came from such different worlds.

At the same time, she felt selfish. Jarron had undoubtedly known that she would be unwilling to leave her family, but if he became Amish so he could marry her, he'd be leaving his own family. While he could still hold a position at his father's farm, that was only assuming that his father wasn't so disappointed about the choice he had made to become Plain. She wasn't even sure if Jarron had even thought about that solution, anyway. She would have been willing to make sacrifices to Jarron, but giving up her faith and family, the only things that had remained constant in her life throughout these past years of struggle, might be too much for her to handle.

One thing was certain: She had to find Jarron.

"Fear not, for I am with you; be not dismayed, for I am your God; I will strengthen you, I will help you, I will uphold you with my righteous right hand." Isaiah 41:10

After the service, Mamm, Daed, and Martha all stayed after to speak with the Bishop, who welcomed Martha back with open arms. Sarah reunited with her husband and children, happy to be among them again, and Emma searched the crowd for Jarron. She strode over to where Sarah was holding her daughter, Ruthie.

"Sarah, have you seen Jarron anywhere?" she asked, trying not to sound panicked.

Sarah shook her head. "Not since last week. Why?"

Before Emma could answer, Sarah's husband Jeremiah leaned forward. "I heard he's packing up to leave again. That's the word in town, at least."

Jeremiah worked for an Englischer company in town, so he often knew all the news. Emma stared at him for a moment, blinked, and turned around without another word, hearing Sarah's concerned voice call after her. She ignored her sister, her chest growing ice cold. Perhaps Jarron truly had decided to run away again, especially after revealing so much of himself to her.

I can't let him go, she thought, tears filling her eyes. Jarron had been her friend for many years, but he had also been gone so much— she couldn't bear to lose someone else who she loved like this, not again.

"Emma, are you feeling okay?"

She turned a little to find Jeremiah staring at her. She could see Sarah staring over at them, concern etched on her face as she tried finishing up a conversation with someone who was fawning over Ruthie.

"*Niet*, Jeremiah." Her breath caught in her throat, and she forced herself to speak. She would not let Jarron leave her again, not without an explanation. "I need you to take me somewhere. Can you do that, for me?"

"Of course, let me just gather up everyone..."

Emma latched onto his arm, trying not to let the desperation creep into her voice. "Mamm and Daed have their buggy here and can take the others home. Please, Jeremiah. I need to get to town, right now."

Jeremiah looked back at Sarah, then back at Emma, clearly torn. Finally,

after what seemed like an eternity, he nodded at Emma. "Okay, let's

go."

"A new commandment I give to you, that you love one another: just as I have loved you, you also are to love one another." - Corinthians 13:13

Pleasant, fat snowflakes fell as they reached town nearly twenty minutes later, but Emma had no time to enjoy the weather. As they approached the Williamses workplace, Emma could already see Jarron's big red truck in the parking lot.

"Right here is fine, Jeremiah. I'll walk the rest of the way," she said.

Before Jeremiah could protest she was out of the carriage, stumbling through the snow. *Please, Lord*, she prayed. *I don't know if this is Your will, but please, let Jarron still be here.* If she could just talk to him, at least to say goodbye—tears filled her eyes at that thought, but she wouldn't force Jarron to stay with her. She loved him, enough to let him go if that was what he needed and wanted.

She slipped on some ice as she reached the snow-laden dirt of the parking lot, nearly falling backwards. Suddenly she felt a strong hand grip her elbow, steadying her.

"Jarron!" she panted. She hadn't even noticed him in the midst of her thoughts, but here he stood before her, the snow casting a white sheen over his clothes.

"Emma, what the heck are you doing here?" he asked, clearly surprised.

"You weren't at service." She struggled to catch her breath through her exertion and emotion. "I had to find you before you left..."

"Left? Em, I was just getting ready to go and meet up with you," he said, confused.

"With me? But..." She searched his eyes, trying to find some sort of deception within them. Finding none, she continued. "But everyone was saying that you were packing up, leaving town..."

"I am packing up," he told her, grabbing her bare hands in his gloved ones. "I'm moving in with Bishop Amos."

"Bishop..."

"Em, I told you I need you, that I want to marry you. I know you'd never want to leave your family, and I'm not going to ask you to. The fact is, I love you. I'm willing to do whatever it takes for you."

"You mean..."

He gave her a grin, kissing her forehead gently at her bewilderment. "Yes, Em. I'm going to become Amish. We're going to get married, if that's alright with you."

She gaped at him, hardly able to control her wildly beating heart. "Jarron..." She shook her head, trying to clear her muddled thoughts. "What about your family?"

Jarron shrugged. "My dad knows that I've been battling with this decision for years, and not just because of you. Bishop Amos has spoken to me on more than one occasion, making me want to know the Lord better. I really think this is Gott's will."

"But... I... Well..."

"Does that mean yes?" he guessed, grinning in amusement at her struggle.

"Yes, oh yes!" she said, jumping into his arms. "I love you, Jarron Williams. I want to be your wife."

He grinned, glancing over to where Jeremiah was waiting in the buggy before laughing, giving Emma a kiss on the cheek that made her glow with happiness. "You've just made me the happiest man on earth, Em."

Made in the USA
Middletown, DE
19 February 2017